THE FLYING DRAGON

THE FLYING DRAGON

Georges Ugeux

ARCHWAY
PUBLISHING

Archway Publishing books may be ordered through booksellers or by contacting:

Archway Publishing
1663 Liberty Drive
Bloomington, IN 47403
www.archwaypublishing.com
1 (888) 242-5904

Because of the dynamic nature of the Internet, any web addresses or
links contained in this book may have changed since publication and
may no longer be valid. The views expressed in this work are solely those
of the author and do not necessarily reflect the views of the publisher,
and the publisher hereby disclaims any responsibility for them.

Any people depicted in stock imagery provided by Thinkstock are models,
and such images are being used for illustrative purposes only.
Certain stock imagery © Thinkstock.

ISBN: 978-1-4808-1856-9 (sc)
ISBN: 978-1-4808-1854-5 (hc)
ISBN: 978-1-4808-1855-2 (e)

Library of Congress Control Number: 2015914290

Print information available on the last page.

Archway Publishing rev. date: 10/29/2015

This book is dedicated to Guiqin Liao, YuanYuan Li, Diana Yang, actress Zhang Ziyi and pianist Yuja Wang, who have inspired the creation of Victoria Leung, the beautiful, strong and moving central character of The Flying Dragon.

1

The crowd around the Hong Kong Arts Center seemed happy as they streamed out of the concert by talented Chinese pianist Yuja Wang. They enthusiastically shared their impressions about her beauty, musicality, and talent. Some of the patrons had seen videos of Yuja Wang playing Chopin at the age of six. Victoria Leung was so in sync with the music she had played tonight: Schubert's impromptus. She also felt so close to the pianist, who commanded the keyboard and seemed on the verge of tears when the third impromptu moved from lightness to depth and passion. At twenty-seven, Yuja Wang was one of the best-known pianists of her generation and now lived in the United States. She had the same drive, intensity, and grace as Victoria herself.

The Center's superb architecture had always given Victoria pleasure. It was modern without ostentation, and its acoustics were close to perfect. Over the years, classical music had increasingly been a source of inspiration in the Chinese world, and the public was ecstatic. For a Chinese pianist to reach this level of excellence and artistry was a source of pride.

Since she had left the financial fraud department of the Hong Kong Police Force, Victoria Leung had enjoyed the freedom attached to her new status of senior detective at Pegasus, an international firm headquartered in London. She intended to fully enjoy this period of her life. Having a family was not on her agenda. Like most thirty-six-year-old women, though, she was starting to give it some thought. Her biological clock inexorably ticked. She knew it. But at the same time, she didn't know what to do about that reality.

Victoria was an assertive and attractive young woman well aware of the impact she had on the male-dominated financial world of Greater China. She had initially faced difficulty demonstrating her leadership and competence, partly because of her good looks, femininity, and youth. She had learned to turn these qualities into assets that she used subtly and wisely. While she remained vulnerable to some aggressive behavior from male colleagues, she knew how to garner respect. Her body was slim and strong; she exercised regularly. She liked having the freedom to wear dresses and skirts rather than a police uniform. But what struck everybody who met her was the power of her demeanor and her smile, which revealed her complexity.

***

Wearing a short red dress, Victoria drank her green tea as she peered through the glass of her office windows into the Hong Kong morning: Kowloon Bay on one side and the old British Empire buildings and parks at the center of Hong Kong on the other. The traffic was penetrating and created an impression of energy and intensity. Hong Kong was not a city for the fainthearted. Victoria was an early bird, and relished the atmosphere of the office before anybody else was in. She was in control and serene.

Victoria looked down at the document on her desk:

> *Henry Chang is in danger. I urgently need to meet you. Meet me at 9:00 a.m. at the Mandarin Oriental for coffee. I desperately need your help. —Diana Y.*

Victoria was stunned. For Diana Yu to send such a dramatic

message was unusual. Henry Chang was Diana's former lover until he broke it off and publicly humiliated her. Now, Diana was asking Victoria to help the bastard. It didn't add up. Did Diana still have feelings for him? Victoria hoped not, but it was the only explanation that made sense.

She sighed. If it had been Chang asking, Victoria would have said no. But Diana was a dear friend. If she was willing to swallow her pride and ask for help, then the least Victoria could do was find out why.

Diana Yu and Victoria had started together at the Hong Kong Police Force. Soon after, Henry Chang became Diana's boyfriend. While she had given the relationship all she had, she was never sure whether Henry was playing or being earnest. Unexpectedly, after they had dated for a year, he dropped her for a Hong Kong socialite, Helena Lee. He then became head of the fixed-income department of the Bank of Hong Kong and Shanghai, or BHS.

The breakup had been particularly painful for Diana since Henry had been cruel enough to do it publicly at a 2012 New Year's party.

Diana was now reaching out through a confidential police cable; whatever had happened to Henry must have been fairly dramatic. The Wan Chai Police headquarters was close to Hong Kong Central and near the Mandarin Oriental Hotel.

2

As HER THOUGHTS WANDERED, VICTORIA HEARD HEAVY FOOT-
steps and noticed a man looking at her from the hallway. Sir Francis
Brian was the head of Pegasus's Hong Kong office. He had been chosen by the firm's executive committee to restore the office's global
stature after an employee was arrested for corruption.

Pegasus had been created by a group of four former MI5 and MI6
top executives who, like most members of secret services around the
world, had been shocked by the attacks of September 11, 2001 and
considered them a wake-up call.

The sober belief that the division among government agencies had
been the main source of this failure because it fragmented intelligence
information and caused agencies to act erratically had led Pegasus's
executives to create their own firm to assist governments, companies, and individuals in countries rife with corruption and terrorism.
Senior detective services contributed to their mission.

What had interested Victoria in leaving the police force and becoming a private detective (besides the pay raise) was the freedom
that private detectives enjoyed in handling their investigations—
within the confines of the law, of course. She had found Sir Francis
incredibly clever, sensitive, and interesting, and she believed working

with him would greatly increase her professional capabilities. His reputation for integrity and sound judgment was renowned, so even if Victoria decided to leave Pegasus after a few years, she reasoned that she would have acquired seniority in her profession.

During Pegasus's search for a senior detective, Victoria's name was mentioned several times, but generally with the comment that she was exceptional, but, you know . . . she was young and a woman. Could she cope? While those prejudices were common in Hong Kong, Sir Francis had had the opportunity to work with female detectives fairing difficult circumstances at the London headquarters, and he respected their courage, skill, judgment, and abilities to contribute to the resolution of complex cases.

Victoria and Sir Francis had now been working together for almost two years. She knew he appreciated her professionalism—and her femininity. She could extract information from suspects by deftly using a combination of her intuition and her sex-appeal.

She turned to him. "I received a cable from the Hong Kong Police Force. It came from Diana Yu, a former colleague at the fraud department." She handed it to him.

After reading it, he asked, "Do you know Henry Chang?"

Victoria briefly explained that he was the head of fixed-income operations at BHS, thinking it unnecessary to talk about his personal relationship with Diana, even though she had met Henry socially on multiple occasions.

Sir Francis sensed that she was only giving him part of the story, but he had enough information and decided not to push Victoria further. "It's an unusual procedure, but I see no reason why you shouldn't meet Diana. Her request seems legitimate. Should you get involved with the police beyond this meeting, I would like to be informed. As you know, we need to handle them with care."

Victoria looked through the window and saw that it would be one of those gorgeous spring days that made Hong Kong a true gem.

As she searched for the latest news on Henry, she learned that he had always been with BHS. He had gotten his MBA at the London Business School, where he had completed the joint strategy and leadership program of the MIT Sloan School of Management.

A series of articles related to the death of Bertrand Wilmington, head of derivatives at BHS, drew her attention. He had fallen from the twenty-second floor of the firm's headquarters. The Hong Kong Police Force had concluded that his death was a suicide.

As Victoria walked to her appointment, she was still puzzled by the strangeness of the message Diana had sent. Had Victoria missed something?

3

As Victoria entered the lobby of the Mandarin Oriental Hotel, she was happy with the quietness of the place. This kind of luxury was from another century, and while the number of modern luxury hotels had mushroomed in Hong Kong, the hotel continued to attract a select clientele of professional guests looking for the special feeling of a home away from home that an older hotel offered. The high ceilings and chandeliers gave it an air of Old England, and the sofas and chairs were of a style straight out of *Downton Abbey*. The attentive staff knew how to make guests comfortable.

Victoria climbed the stairs to the mezzanine without even looking at the lobby, as the mezzanine was one of her and Diana's preferred retreats. As Victoria ordered an orange juice, Diana appeared in her navy blue suit. Victoria had always been struck by Diana's strict style.

Diana spoke fast and sometimes brutally, especially when unfairly contradicted. She wasn't inclined to compromise when that happened. Although this habit had made her some enemies, Diana was passionate and had a great sense of humor—just like Victoria. Today, she appeared more serene, but Victoria knew that this was just a facade. Victoria saw profound distress in her eyes, even though Diana hid it well.

Victoria asked her what she wanted to drink, and she ordered jasmine green tea.

"It is so good to see you again," Diana told her friend. "I am so glad you could come. This case has been torturing me for the last week."

"I was surprised to receive your cable," Victoria said. "It's official. Did you stay in touch with Henry? You're the last person I would have expected to contact me about him."

"Not at all. I hate him deeply for what he did to me and won't forgive him. But he reached out to me in desperation. Did you see what happened at BHS?"

"The suicide story?"

"The guy who allegedly committed suicide, Bertrand Wilmington, was a colleague of Henry's. Henry's position was more senior than Bertrand's, but they had the relationship of peers."

"Why would Henry be involved in a suicide case? That seems so bizarre."

"In the absence of other evidence, ruling the case a suicide was the easy decision, but it might not tell the whole story. Henry called me to ask whether the police would reopen the inquiry. He believes that Bertrand was pushed—if not physically, then emotionally—by one of his colleagues."

"Do you believe the suicide theory?"

"I asked the criminal department to look into it, but they refused to reopen the investigation. They're happy with the current categorization, and so is BHS's inspection department. I asked Henry if I could reach out to you, and he agreed. He feels threatened professionally and personally by the possible backlash at BHS."

"Why don't you tell me what you know?"

Bertrand Wilmington was born in 1982 and raised in England. His father was a diplomat and his mother a writer. He was sent to a Catholic boarding school at the age of twelve, while his father was assigned to foreign embassies. During that period, Bertrand suffered from home-sickness, as English boarding schools did not often protect students from emotional distress. He had discovered his homosexuality during a summer camp a couple of years after beginning his studies at the school.

At university, Bertrand befriended a Chinese boy, Louis Cheung, who was a year younger. They became passionate lovers. However, Bertrand did not confine his sexual encounters to men, and his experiences with women were rich and profoundly tender. He also cultivated friendships with women, who had told him that he sometimes understood women better than straight guys did. Diana Yu had actually met him through cultural activities in Hong Kong. They both were particularly passionate about all kinds of music and dance.

Louis and Bertrand applied together to join BHS for internships. During their internships, Bertrand became interested in derivative products and applied for an analyst position on the derivatives trading desk. He quickly became effective and knowledgeable, and money and excitement drove his professional aspirations. Louis preferred the investors' side and had joined BHS's hedge fund.

Bertrand kept his sex life discreet until he received a strange voice message from David Chen, the head of the back office, who had heard about his proclivities through a friend of Louis Cheung's and asked Bertrand out. The end of the message was unambiguous: "Let's have the same fun you had with Louis." Bertrand politely refused.

David persisted, so Bertrand told him directly that he would not entertain sexual relationships with colleagues. The meeting was stormy, and if David's secretary, Olivia Shuler, had not interrupted it for a call, it might have ended much worse.

A few days later, some strange trades were booked on Bertrand's client's account. He questioned the back office, and a young accoun-tant told him that those trades had been input from BHS proprietary account 1130-01 and authorized by David Chen. Each time Bertrand tried to cancel them, they were reinstated.

He decided to ask Henry Chang if this had ever happened to him. Henry told him that only two people could use that account—John Highbridge, the head of the proprietary trading desk, or David Chen. Trades like these applied directly to the clients' account were prohibited, as banks could not mix their own activities with those of clients.

Henry then called John Highbridge, who denied originating the transactions but promised to look into the matter.

A week after, a HK$50 million position was booked in a Chinese account, and Bertrand received a voice mail message: "If you don't want to play with me tonight, I will push you out. Don't talk about it with Henry if you want to survive." It was David Chen's voice. Bertrand decided to inform the audit department.

But Bertrand first called Henry Chang, who was in Shanghai, to inform him of the events. After Bertrand relayed the voice mail message, Henry told him that he was right to be worried and asked Bertrand to come to his office as soon as Henry got back from Shanghai. They would go to compliance together.

They met and decided to clean Bertrand's trading book with David Chen and John Highbridge after the closing of markets. Since the trades were irregular, they needed to be reversed to their situations prior to the transaction. A day later, Bertrand was found dead by the BHS security team in the back courtyard of the building.

As Diana recounted the story, she seemed on the verge of tears. She went silent when she reached the end of the story. Victoria could see how the open wound Henry Chang had inflicted on Diana had played a part in her sympathy for Henry's situation and her feelings about Bertrand's death.

Victoria broke the silence: "What was Henry looking for in going to you? Knowing that you work for the fraud office and might reach out to me made that a bold and unusual move. He can't predict our conclusions. Does he realize that?"

"He told me that, directly or indirectly, Bertrand's death was provoked. He was shattered by the fact that he hadn't recognized the gravity of the situation when Bertrand called him during his trip to Shanghai."

"Why is he so concerned? It's hard to believe that his first objective would be concern for Bertrand Wilmington. He must have a stake in this. Henry is such a narcissist."

"He is. It means that BHS either didn't do its internal inquiry or didn't consider the findings worthy of the police's attention—the usual self-protection reflex of bankers. They hate bad publicity."

Victoria smiled, remembering her own experience in investment banking, where no whistle-blower rights existed and a layer of confidentiality always covered bad news. In Asia, the risk of losing face could be poisonous.

Victoria had joined Pegasus's financial fraud department in 2007 after having spent five years in investment banking with the powerful China International Trust and Investment Company—CITIC—in Hong Kong. As part of the bank's internal audit department, she had seen up close and personal the behaviors of those she called "the sharks," traders who didn't always play by the rules. That experience had inspired her to pursue a career chasing financial fraud.

"Is there anything you can do?" Diana asked.

"I'll ask Sir Francis whether Pegasus can accept the assignment and if I can personally handle the case. If the case were to inflate, he might reach out to BHS's general counsel, Sir Francis's former colleague from the board of the British Chamber of Commerce in Hong Kong."

"Can you start without involving BHS?"

"At first, yes. I can meet Henry at my office after lunch. I assume you won't want to attend."

Victoria didn't like Henry, but Diana was her friend, and the case was interesting. BHS might not be too pleased that she was playing in their sandbox, but Sir Francis and Harvey Lee were old friends, so Sir Francis would be able to smooth any ruffled feathers.

"Thanks, Vic. It means a lot."

"Do you still love Henry?"

Diana smiled. She had been asking herself the same question. "No, I don't. He hurt me too deeply. But I'm still jealous. I cannot stand the pictures of him flirting with Helena Lee and going to parties. Have you seen her pictures at the Cannes Film Festival? She was half naked. We women can get so deeply attached to men, but they don't deserve our attachment. They are butterflies."

"Some men are exceptions, but Henry certainly fits that description."

Victoria had been through a similar experience when she was twenty-one, so she could relate to her friend's pain. Betrayal was the worst feeling anyone could experience. She shook off those thoughts and hugged her friend for a long moment before they parted. Victoria wanted to know what had really happened at BHS. The suicide explanation had been an easy one, and she knew better than anybody that it would be a challenge to make the police force change its opinion.

4

The morning after Bertrand's death, BHS President for Asia John Wilcox summoned the key executives to a meeting. He looked disturbed as he entered the room.

"I have sad news for all of us. Bertrand Wilmington jumped to his death from the twenty-second floor around 2:00 a.m. today. We found a note on his desk that really stunned me. It read, 'Better to leave than to suffer daily humiliation in a suffocating and bullying trading room.' Does anybody know anything about what could have prompted this apparent suicide?"

John Wilcox was an honest man and was sincere about his feelings. He had often repeated to his direct reports that he would never tolerate a threatening or bullying environment at BHS. He asked clearly whether anybody knew of anything that could have led Bertrand to commit suicide. If anyone did, that person needed to talk to John Wilcox directly or to General Counsel Harvey Lee. Additionally, he reminded his employees to use the firm's ombudsman channel to communicate internal information that might contradict corporate policies—a rare invitation to whistle-blowing. A memo would be sent within an hour.

David Chen stared at Henry Chang. How much did Henry know

about David's bullying and sexual harassment of Bertrand? The previous evening, they had corrected the HK$50 million position they had transferred from the proprietary account the day before. Would Henry report it? Could he stop Henry from doing so?

That afternoon, Henry Chang met with John Wilcox and Harvey Lee and asked to be considered a whistle-blower and protected as such. Harvey agreed.

Henry began, "Bertrand called me when I was in Shanghai to say he was very depressed to have found a HK$50 million transfer directly from the proprietary account to one of his key accounts from the Chongqing Hedge Fund, against our rules. He was also upset by what he described to me as sexual bullying from David Chen."

"You of course understand the seriousness of what you are disclosing," John said. "I really appreciate your coming forward. I know it's not easy, but this information is valuable. We'll launch a formal internal inquiry. Please remain available if Harvey or I need to talk to you."

Although the bank's senior executives faced extreme pressure from shareholders and regulators, Bertrand's colleagues could not understand why he would have committed suicide. He had been such a friendly and positive colleague. He paid attention to those in the back office and in the front office. He cared about people.

Among these colleagues were Mary Li, the head of audits, and Olivia Shuler. They had a coffee together after the meeting.

"I am deeply disturbed," Olivia said. "There's something that you need to know, as you'll probably be involved in the inquiry. You didn't hear it from me, but you need to understand that David harassed Bertrand for some time in connection with a guy from the University of Hong Kong."

"I knew Bertrand and David were gay. Could this be the reason for Bertrand's death?"

"I can't see David killing him. But he can be quite brutal. You've seen it."

"Everybody I've spoken to has said the same thing: they don't believe that he could commit suicide. We'll need to act quickly to avoid suspicion. Please let me know if you observe anything abnormal," requested Mary.

"I definitely will. I'm truly saddened. I had a good working relationship with Bertrand, and he was sweet to me. I really hope we will find out the truth."

More than anything, Bertrand's death was met with incredulity and sadness.

However, one colleague felt differently. David Chen was a bully. He should have been fired for having almost strangled one of his employees. It had happened in the middle of the financial crisis, and a trader had just been moved to the settlement department to reinforce the team. The trader had made the classic mistake of confusing two accounts, and the employee had gone straight to the trader to resolve the problem.

"Who do you think you are?" David had berated the employee. "Don't you know that nobody can call traders without my permission? I'll break your neck."

He violently shook the employee by the shoulders and then clasped his hands around the man's neck. "You're suffocating me!" the employee gasped.

David might have killed the employee had Olivia Shuler not seen this and called the security department. Two black-belt guards rushed in, took David to the ground in two strokes, and held him on the floor.

In most cases, aggression like Henry's would have led to one's termination. But as the head of the back office, he had enjoyed increased freedom in the way he managed his employees since the global financial crisis. David enjoyed his power and was not shy to use it for his own interests.

5

VICTORIA LEUNG WALKED BACK TO HER OFFICE FEELING BOTH disturbed and moved by the situation, not as much because of the investigation as the memories of her experience at CITIC.

When she had joined the CITIC, her role was to ensure that the confirmation of client orders matched the traders' positions in real time. It looked simple enough, but it required attention to detail and speed. To make the situation more complex, the orders were often cancelled and reentered the same day.

She soon discovered that the pressure from upstairs was strong, multiform, and pervasive. Traders believed themselves to be the rulers. The first time Victoria revealed an anomaly between two trades that had given her the impression of manipulation, she got a call from the head trader of US securities, Dick Wilson, an American who had been at CITIC for five years.

He was arrogant and convinced that nobody would ever sanction him since his desk was so profitable. He had even managed to stop attempts to reduce the basis of the bonus pool for the team (from which he always took 50 percent).

"How long have you done this job, Vic?" he asked.

"I joined the audit department ten months ago. And my name is Victoria, not Vic."

"What are you in charge of in the audit department?"

"The US equity business."

"Did you know that the previous girl in charge of audit of the US equity book left abruptly?"

"I heard she left for health reasons."

"That's one way to put it. She was a bit too curious about some positions, so we made sure she wouldn't resist the upstairs pressure. She held up until we crushed her."

"What do you mean?"

"We made her life miserable. She was even harassed at home."

"I will still do my job."

"We are the people who make money, and the audit staff will never stop that from happening. We have our rules."

"What do you mean, 'our rules'? Are they different from those we follow in the audit department?"

"Our rules are simple: make money. Okay?"

"Whatever it takes?"

"I already got rid of three auditors from my book in the last five years."

"I get the message," Victoria said. "But I'm not going to take it."

"You'll learn who the bosses are here. A young chick like you is easy to destroy."

"Bullying won't work on me. If you have a good explanation for this trade, please inform the settlement department."

"You really don't get it. And on top of that, you are a cutie. Watch yourself, baby. I will find you somewhere, sometime."

"You seem to consider yourself above the rules, so I will certainly watch any discrepancies in your book carefully. Thanks for the lead."

What Victoria hated above all was the attitude of entitlement of the traders, who considered the settlement, compliance, and audit staff a nuisance they needed to weaken. This led to intolerable behavior that few firms were able to redress because they couldn't afford to risk driving traders away. Often enough, management preferred to let it go unpunished. Yet, scandals could take down a firm, as had happened to Baring Brothers in Singapore when a rogue trader managed to take control of the back office.

As she recalled the incident with Dick Wilson, Victoria's heart beat fast. She had felt completely shattered when it happened. She deeply hated this upstairs-downstairs mentality, and it was one of the reasons she had accepted the offer to join the fraud department of the Hong Kong Police Force.

Many years later, following Facebook's disastrous IPO, when the price collapsed by fifty percent during the first days of trading, the Hong Kong Securities and Futures Commission, (SFC) at the request of their US colleagues at the Securities Exchange Commission, (SEC) reached out to CITIC to interrogate Dick Wilson about his purchase of one hundred thousand Facebook shares. CITIC had underwritten them at market price, and Dick had deposited them into his own account in New York. The problem was that Dick had retransferred the position at the issue price to the CITIC proprietary account from his own account after the price decreased by fifty percent. By doing so, he had avoided a personal loss of $2.5 million that CITIC incurred instead.

The enforcement department of the SFC accepted the presence of an SEC inspector. Dick trembled as the evidence was presented to him. He fought like hell, maintaining it was an error on a difficult day. Ultimately, the SEC provided a copy of an e-mail Dick had sent to his US broker: "That's one for us and not for CITIC. Cheers. Fifty-fifty as usual."

The broker had answered: "Are you mad? This is against all the rules, and the SEC is all over the Facebook IPO."

The broker returned the transfer, but it was too late. The internal audit department already had the evidence. When the FBI interrogated the broker, he pleaded guilty and agreed to cooperate. Dick

Wilson eventually faced facts and tendered his resignation. He was banned from the financial industry.

Victoria smiled when her successor, Mary Li, gave her this news. Justice had prevailed, at least this time.

6

VICTORIA WAS TRYING TO APPLY HER EXPERIENCE WITH THE TRADing room to the case of Bertrand Wilmington when she entered the lobby of the Singga Center and took the elevator to the Pegasus offices on the thirty-fifth floor. In her office, a message slip told her that Henry Chang had called fifteen minutes ago. She needed a coffee before returning the call, so she went to the pantry and fixed a double Nespresso. She lingered there for a minute before going to Sir Francis's office.

He welcomed her with his usual, "Hello, Miss Victoria," and invited her to sit on the sofa. She chose the chair opposite his desk instead—she didn't want him to be distracted by the view he'd get of her short dress if she sat on the sofa.

"How was your meeting with Diana?" Sir Francis asked.

"It went well," Victoria answered. "She was emotional about the whole situation. She truly wants to help Henry Chang. She was overwhelmed that he had reached out to her."

"What was the matter?"

"Do you remember the BHS suicide case from two weeks ago?"

"Yes, I do. I thought it was a usual case of suicide in banking. Didn't the police treat it that way? And what does that have to do with Henry Chang?"

"Henry was a senior colleague of the man who allegedly committed suicide. He had reached out to Henry a few hours before his death. Henry believes there is more to the case than the reported suicide and wants to hire Pegasus to get to the bottom of it."

"Do you believe there's something to the case?"

"I'm not sure yet," Victoria replied. "However, my experience with trading rooms leads me to question the bank's and the police's quick conclusion. They both have an interest in keeping foul play quiet."

"What do you have in mind?"

"There's evidence of possible trading manipulation and sexual harassment. The victim was gay."

Sir Francis acknowledged the mix of personal and professional motives but reminded Victoria that it was unusual for an individual to hire Pegasus. "What would his homosexuality have to do with BHS?"

"Bertrand was apparently bullied by a colleague when he found evidence that the colleague might have corrupted his trading book."

"A crime of passion?"

"It's too early for me to choose a direction, but there are some troubling facts I'll speak to Henry this afternoon, and then I'll be able to tell you more about it."

"Keep me posted. Your experience might be critical to resolving this case, assuming that there is a case."

Victoria particularly appreciated that Sir Francis gave her ownership of her work and the security essential to do it well.

She returned to her office with a sense of unease, though. This was only the beginning of an inquiry that would take her deeper into the trading underworld. It would be complex and hugely political. Her experience with Sun Hung Kai properties told her as much. And now, Victoria no longer enjoyed the protection and resources of the police.

She also felt apprehensive about dealing with Henry Chang. The conversation might not be easy.

She ate a salad at her desk while looking for recent information related to the case. It had left the media's focus almost immediately, but a report in the *South China Morning Post* struck her.

Feng Wang, the well-respected economics editor, had written it the weekend before. Interestingly, it hadn't been published in the print edition, only online. Was the story not interesting enough or too sensitive to reach the print edition? At that level, journalists knew much more than they published. She was asking herself that question when her phone rang.

7

"Hello, Victoria, it's Henry Chang," he said joyfully. "It's been a long time since we've met or spoken."

Victoria couldn't believe his detachment. A death—possibly a murder—had occurred so close to him. Was he completely in denial?

"I understand Diana updated you about my concerns. I'm in the neighborhood of the Singga building, and I was wondering whether we could meet this afternoon."

"You are welcome here."

Too many things had happened over the last twelve hours. Victoria needed to prepare. Opening her computer, she Googled Henry to try to understand him more thoroughly. All she knew of him was filtered through her own experience and what she knew of the way he had treated Diana Yu. She needed more objective facts.

As she looked further, she found a notice of his purchase of a four-thousand-square-foot apartment in Mayfair, an area of London. He had bought it in 2003, near the height of the market: £4 million was a hefty price. He had bought it when he was working in London. He certainly had become wealthy. The apartment was now worth at least three times what he had paid for it.

Victoria hadn't seen Henry since the infamous New Year's Eve party of 2012. And now she was meeting him as a client of Pegasus at Diana's request. Life had a strange way of coming full circle.

At 3:30 p.m. sharp, Victoria's secretary, Judy Wang, announced that Henry Chang had arrived. Victoria went to the waiting room and looked Henry over before he noticed her. He was unchanged: well dressed and remarkably relaxed. Despite his unforgivable treatment of her friend, Victoria thought him handsome and had been sensitive to his charm. She took a deep breath, chased away those thoughts, and went straight to him.

She led him to a meeting room and Judy offered him something to drink. He declined politely.

"I heard about the death of Bertrand Wilmington. It is horrible and must have affected you. How close were you?" Victoria asked when Judy had left.

"As you know, those of us in fixed income need to work closely with the derivative department. We're often subject to the same underlying security, even though we run separate trading books," He paused and smiled at her, clearly trying to give the conversation a more personal tone. "We have a lot more in common than you might think."

Is he trying to flirt with me? Victoria asked herself. He would never stop trying to seduce.

"So, Bertrand and I had regular contact," Henry continued. "Once in a while we would go out for a drink. We weren't exactly friends, but I was his mentor."

Henry Chang, a mentor? Now that's news. How could this self-centered bastard mentor anybody?

"When he called me in Shanghai, his tone was less assertive than usual. It could have been anything, you know. I didn't pay much attention to it. I regret that very much now."

Now we're getting somewhere. Does he realize how ridiculous he's being? "What exactly did he tell you on the phone?" Victoria asked.

"He was concerned that David Chen was using the proprietary book to force him into a sexual relationship. Bertrand had found a HK$50 million proprietary position irregularly transferred to one of his clients. He asked if he should go straight to compliance."

"Did you know about the transfer before the conversation?"

"It was the first time he had informed me of this breach of the rules."

"What did you tell him?"

"I said we should look at the situation together with David Chen and John Highbridge when I got back."

Victoria stared at him with incredulously. A large position was transferred against the rules, and they had to ask whether they needed to go to compliance? Were they hoping to hide that major irregularity on their own first?

"We would have gone to compliance if the situation was still unresolved. I wasn't comfortable letting him go straight there without me. He was too emotional on the phone."

"Why were you uncomfortable? Did you suspect collusion between traders and the back office?"

"Possibly. That's why I wanted Diana to contact you. You know the business and the culture and might be able to find out exactly what happened. You were in audit, I believe."

"Yes, I was. Do you want to hire Pegasus for an investigation of the books?"

"No, I want you to take the case from the beginning and examine it holistically. There are too many elements that are unclear. I trust your ability to sort out the Gordian knot, without cutting it!"

Is he hoping to fool me? Victoria thought. She wasn't certain he really wanted to resolve the case but didn't doubt his sincerity.

"Is homosexuality part of the equation?" she asked.

"Diana must have told you that David Chen, the head of our back office, had approached Bertrand to force him into a relationship that he had told David he didn't want."

"How long have you known this?"

"Probably three months?"

"How did you protect Bertrand?"

"Protect Bertrand? I'm not a babysitter."

"Why did you not go to David to ask him to stop? You're the most senior executive in the fixed-income department, if I'm not mistaken."

"Yes, but I didn't believe I should get involved in personal matters."

"Personal matters? You must be joking," Victoria said angrily. "Harassment of any nature is against rules and regulations. Are you not responsible for enforcing them? If you were shirking your duties, it will appear in the case if it's reopened."

Henry's face showed he was frightened by her ferocity. If Victoria's eyes could shoot arrows, he would be a dead man. Seeing him disoriented, Victoria decided to push him further.

"Why are you interested in finding the truth, Henry? From what I remember, you are not exactly a Good Samaritan, except when it comes to young, beautiful women. Did you call compliance?"

"Bertrand and I had already had meetings related to a proprietary trade a few days before his death."

"Shouldn't he have informed the group head of derivatives in London, where all positions are managed?"

"I didn't think it was big enough, and I thought it could be better resolved locally. He only realized the risks when the transaction appeared on his book having been sold to one of his clients."

Victoria was flabbergasted. She had thought that perhaps Henry's request to hire Pegasus had been emotional, but it turned out that he just wanted to cover himself, with her help. Now that Bertrand was dead, all his complacencies could be exposed. Could that have been a motive for Henry to have killed Bertrand Wilmington?

"Did you tell Bertrand that he had to report the trade?"

"I didn't think about it at the time. You know, I trade securities.

I'm not a derivatives expert. I don't exactly know the compliance rules that govern those guys."

Victoria couldn't believe David's credulity. How could he believe that she would swallow this explanation with her background in audit?

She yelled, "You can bullshit your colleagues, Henry, but you cannot bullshit me, and you know it. I can only help you if you are honest with me. Is that clear? Why did you call Diana on this matter? Have you not hurt her enough? You could have called me directly. You knew perfectly well that getting the police involved would require a lot of work and persuasion. She was caught between her duty and her attachment to you."

"I know, but there was nobody else I knew who could understand what I was going through. I couldn't possibly talk to friends or people in the bank, let alone to Helena. And I wasn't sure how you would have reacted."

"Don't play with Diana's emotions if you want me on the investigation. If anything happens to her, I will make sure Pegasus drops the case."

How could Diana have ever thought that Henry could love her? He was so fake, and now maybe even be a criminal. Victoria switched her focus back to the trading side of the affair.

"Do you have access to the trading room and the systems during the night?"

"Yes, I do. Why?"

"Can you let me in? I'm trying to figure out how the proprietary positions that ended up in Bertrand's client account could be activated and by whom. It might take a few hours. I can start on Monday at 7:00 p.m. Does that work for you?"

Henry was clearly scared that Victoria might uncover some delicate information if she did a forensic audit of Bertrand's book. He and Bertrand were in charge of a few critical accounts for Mainland institutions.

"Well, there is a risk," Henry said. "Let me see if I can get you a badge as an IT advisor to fixed income. There is no way you could get in without security clearance. We might need to be accompanied by a staff member from compliance."

"I actually wouldn't mind having a bodyguard from compliance when we're together," Victoria said with a smile. She couldn't resist a brief moment of flirtation. "I can't be sure how you'll behave."

You are too cute, Victoria, Henry thought to himself. *I'll make sure you are being escorted.* "Let me see what I can do. I will let you know."

"I'll send you the contract to officially hire Pegasus," Victoria was all business. "I look forward to finding out what or who is behind this."

"Me too."

Henry approached Victoria and, in one quick movement, grabbed her by the shoulders to kiss her. Immediately, Victoria reacted, giving him her best black-belt torsion. A second later, Henry was on the ground.

"You are *my* client," she said sharply, completely taken aback. "And this is a professional relationship. Am I clear?"

8

Victoria went back to her office and peered out the window.

There was a demonstration on the street protesting the announcement that Beijing would vet the candidates for the next election in Hong Kong. This had infuriated students, and they were making their feelings known.

The police soon arrived in force. Hong Kong didn't like confronting Beijing. Despite its complex political structure, Hong Kong was, and still is, the international center of Chinese capital markets.

When the treaty giving ownership of Hong Kong to the United Kingdom expired, China maintained Hong Kong's economic model. Beijing needed a window to the world and, more importantly, a convertible and widely accepted currency—the Hong Kong dollar.

The conversation with Henry had left Victoria exhausted. It had brought back intense memories of her negative experiences with manipulative traders. His flirting had also been unbearable, but she was happy to have kept the discussion professional. She might have been the Flying Dragon, but sometimes it hurt.

Victoria first met Henry during industry gatherings and conferences, and they had attended regulatory-training programs together.

She learned then that he was not particularly fond of following the rules. During the classes, he played with his BlackBerry and sent text messages to women in the room. He often flirted with her. At the time, she was shy and confused about her feelings toward men and avoided him, even though she found him good-looking.

On the evening of the final day of the class, they had gone to a bar in downtown Hong Kong. She sat next to him as they chatted, and he had tried to fondle her. It would not be the last time.

***

Henry came from a wealthy family involved in the trading world: his father owned one of the most prominent import-export agencies between Hong Kong and Australia. He admired his father's success, but his father was rarely present. His mother also spent most of her time outside the home as the public face of the Chang Shipping Group.

At school, the aura of Henry's family protected him. He was active in sports. He grew tall, and the school's basketball team recruited him. He could shoot with precision from far away, and his height frightened other teams and disturbed their view of the net.

At that point, Henry's father took interest in his son and advised him to study and gather experience in trading so he could join the family business. He also took Henry to visit one of the company's mineral carriers, a profitable business because Hong Kong needed steel from Australia to build skyscrapers but a business that involved not-so insignificant bribing of senior officials in the Hong Kong Port Authority, who "auctioned" berths.

Henry then studied finance at the London Business School and barely succeeded. He was much more interested in hanging out with traders in the city than listening to his professors. He preferred learning the tricks of the business over understanding in-depth knowledge of the market impact of securities.

When he finished his studies, Henry was offered trading positions in investment banking. BHS offered the perfect platform as a dual UK and Hong Kong bank. During the analyst program, the head of fixed income noticed him asking incisive and sharp questions. That evening, he invited Henry to dinner and made him a six-figure offer. Henry was in heaven.

He learned trading in BHS's London and New York offices. When the head of equity in Hong Kong was called back to London, Henry was offered a senior position in the equity-capital markets division to handle the new issues of shares, particularly IPOs in Hong Kong. While he was good at predicting the markets, he never took the time to understand the complexity of equity valuation, so he maneuvered himself to a less intellectually demanding position as deputy head of fixed-income trading. In 2011, he took over his boss's position and took responsibility for BHS's bond-trading operations.

Victoria thought about her deep ambivalence toward Henry Chang.

She thought about why he had chosen to date Diana Yu. She offered him deep and caring love that few men realized was a genuine treasure but without which they were often lost. Yet, she was strong and required respect. Maybe he couldn't stand her resistance to his arrogance. Henry was a player and a professional gambler.

Then, on New Year's Eve 2012, they went to a party at the top of the Shangri-La. Diana didn't know what to expect, but the party would be her entry into corporate society.

A French colleague, Chantal Guyet, had invited Victoria as well. This would be different from the parties she had attended while with the police. She had bought her first Armani dress: it had spaghetti straps and a rather short hemline without being provocative. As she entered the party, she looked at herself in the mirror and was still worried than she might not be attractive enough. Chantal couldn't convince her otherwise.

They went straight to the dance floor and were quickly joined by a group that included Henry and Diana. They made a gorgeous couple, and Victoria was really happy for Diana—but not without a pinch of jealousy.

When Victoria left the dance floor and headed to the restrooms, she didn't notice that Henry had followed her and abandoned Diana, who was talking to Chantal. Henry grabbed her and clasped his hand over her mouth. For a fleeting moment, as his hand reached between her legs, a desire stirred within her. A moment later, the feeling vanished and Victoria kicked Henry in the groin, leaving him trying not to scream.

It was that night that Henry announced his engagement to Helena Lee in front of everybody, including Diana, who would have collapsed if Chantal and Victoria had not held her up and taken her out of the crowd to a secluded space where she could vent her sadness and anger. The three of them left the party soon after. There was no joy to share.

9

The day had been long enough, so Victoria went to the pool, figuring a swim would be the best antidote to the investigation. After several laps, she left the pool and headed to the locker room in her one-piece white swimsuit feeling refreshed and reenergized.

As Victoria left the shower, she recognized the woman flirting with the swimming instructor: Helena Lee. Having been present at the infamous New Year's party, Victoria was sure that this was the woman who had replaced Diana Yu in Henry Chang's heart.

Helena looked much less attractive in her bikini than she had in photos. Cellulite showed in her thighs, and the surgeon who had enhanced her breasts had failed to keep their natural shape. Women noticed these things, and they could be unforgiving.

After putting on a white robe, Victoria approached Helena and reminded her of when they had met.

"Oh yes, the engagement came as a complete surprise to me. Henry and I had been out a few times before, but I didn't believe he was serious about marrying me. It was wonderful, and I was thrilled. You might have seen me cry."

"I did indeed. It was a very emotional moment. When are you getting married?"

"I thought it would be by the end of the year, but Henry remains vague about it. He seems preoccupied by problems at the office."

"Really. Anything serious?"

"I'm not sure. One of his colleagues committed suicide. He seems to believe that it was because of some bad trades. He takes his job so seriously."

"I'm sorry to hear it. Does it dishearten you?"

"Not really. I'm so focused on my next movie."

"What will it be?"

"It's about the fight between two Prohibition-era gangs in the United States. It's being shot in Bali."

"Why in Bali?"

"The fight apparently happens in America, but shooting in the US is too expensive. The unions have so many conditions, you know. I'm playing the role of the mistress of the boss. It will be spicy. My co-star is sexy, but I'm not allowed to tell you his name. You would probably be jealous. So it should be fun."

"Does that bother Henry?"

"I wish it would. He is such a playboy and a voyeur. Although he has asked to see how those scenes are being filmed but I categorically refused. I knew he was like this before we were engaged. On the other hand, waiting for a faithful husband is the surest condemnation to celibacy, don't you think? See you next time at the pool."

The conversation perplexed Victoria. Helena had consciously taken Henry from another woman, she knew a guy committed suicide, and yet she was acting as if everything was normal. She was probably not a very credible actress, but she was self-absorbed. Frustration and bitterness were not very far away for her. Victoria thought it interesting that Henry had told Helena about Bertrand Wilmington's suicide. That indicated that he was more disturbed than he let on, although it could also be an excuse not to marry Helena. Victoria's impression of Helena had not improved. Had she known she was talking to Henry's detective, she certainly would not have been so talkative.

Victoria went to a bench and looked at the swimming pool. There were definitely more women at the pool than men. A group of eight synchronized swimmers created a flower with their bodies, holding each other's hands. Victoria knew it well, having practiced this routine herself in college. She had competed on the team and had even won a championship in Taiwan. They had the admiration of the entire university.

Victoria's phone rang: it was Diana.

"Hi, Victoria. Where are you?"

"At the swimming pool."

"Did you swim already?"

"Yes."

"Too bad. I would have joined you."

"I'm not sure you would have liked it. Helena Lee is here."

There was a moment of silence. Victoria knew Diana didn't like to be reminded of Helena Lee's existence.

"Wow. Did you talk?"

"Yes, and among other things, she indicated that Henry was disturbed by Bertrand Wilmington's suicide, which he chalked up to bad trades."

"How interesting. Henry isn't exactly the kind of guy to talk about office matters with a lover. How did your conversation with Henry go?"

"Well, I'm still unclear as to what his true motives are, let alone whether he's telling me everything he knows."

"Did you find him candid in his approach?"

"Henry is anything but candid. I thought he was downright disingenuous."

"Do you believe that he feels more at ease with a woman detective?"

"Definitely, but for the wrong reasons. He is convinced he can always seduce a woman or manipulate her." Victoria paused. "Diana, is this the first time he reached out to you since he got engaged?"

A long silence followed, and Victoria guessed Diana was embarrassed. "Not really. I reached out to him to have dinner."

"How did he seem when you spoke to him?"

"He had completely lost a certain ingenuity that had made him charming, and he had become arrogant. He could do nothing wrong. I couldn't really share anything about myself. He was so self-centered that he didn't pay attention to my emotions."

"How did you feel?"

"I wanted to make peace. All he talked about was what was happening at the office. And yet, I was wearing his favorite dress, the one I wore at the New Year's party."

"Did he try to seduce you again?"

"If you can call it seduction. I had to leave before the end of the dinner."

"I'm not surprised," Victoria said. "Did you learn anything about his professional life?"

"Yes. He was up for promotion to the executive committee and was doing everything to get it."

"Could this be why he didn't report irregularities to compliance?"

"Certainly. He avoided all confrontation."

"Would he kill to get that promotion?"

"Probably, if he thought it was necessary." Diana responded, but Victoria could hear a twinge of emotion in her voice.

"Even with all of this going on," Victoria said, "he is still the same Henry when it comes to women. I'd be careful around him and his charm."

"Don't worry about me. I'm not easily influenced," Diana said.

"Are you sure?"

Victoria laughed. She knew Diana well enough to know that she had a soft spot. Despite her composure, she was a romantic. And so was Victoria.

10

THE DAY HAD BEEN FULL OF SURPRISES, AND VICTORIA FELT THAT she had only scratched the surface of this mystery. She couldn't possibly ask Diana what the files of the Hong Kong Police Force contained, but she wondered whether they had really done their due diligence. After one day, she had uncovered several leads that made her question whether the death was really a suicide.

Victoria resolved to find out the reasons behind Bertrand's death and driven by more than professional curiosity. The passionate side of the case touched her, and Diana's and Henry's involvement added spice to the plot.

She took the ferry to Kowloon. She liked this noisy, friendly, dirty place, but her modern apartment granted her some respite.

After the ferry docked, Victoria walked through Nathan Road, which still featured shops selling fresh and healthy food.

"You look worried, Miss Victoria." Over the years, Mr. Lee, the Korean owner of the grocery next to her apartment had found a way to guess Victoria's mood, and he always offered her comfort food. He had a fatherly attitude and cared about her.

"I had a tough day but a good one."

"I have what you need tonight: fresh dumplings and wonderful crabmeat to go with them."

"You read my mind, Mr. Lee."

He dished up a portion to go. "Here it is. Enjoy your meal. And get some sleep."

"Thank you, Mr. Lee. This will make me feel at home."

Victoria changed into her favorite Chinese gown, a light blue number with blossoming tree branches. That robe, bought in Suzhou, gave her a sense of freedom and harmony, comfort and sexiness.

As she prepared the dumplings and the vegetables she had bought, she flipped on her favorite TV series, *Cooking with Ms. Wong.* Victoria had started cooking lessons for fun and was getting good at it. She loved the challenge of harmonizing the ingredients and flavors. She added a few spices suggested by Ms. Wong, who was an expert in spicy cuisines: Chinese, Indian, and Middle Eastern. Hers was the most popular cooking program on Hong Kong television.

Victoria picked up her iPad and searched for the movie Helena Lee was going to shoot in Bali. She would be playing the role of a drug trafficker in love with a dealer. Since she was not shy, it would probably be an active month, Victoria guessed. Her co-star was Malik Zidi, a Frenchman of Middle Eastern origin. He was younger than Helena and definitely handsome. Victoria mused that Helena might not mind a night or two with this man. The thought aroused her, but she chased it away and turned to magazines in search of gossip and fashion news.

Victoria's recruitment to Pegasus had been unusual.

Sir Francis had invited her to the Pierre, the gastronomic restaurant at the Mandarin Oriental Hotel overlooking the bay. Jean Denis Le Bras, who had honed his skills under the tutelage of Pierre

Gagnaire, was considered the best young French chef in Hong Kong. Sir Francis had wanted to impress her.

Victoria's demeanor immediately stunned him when she walked in, and heads turned as she glided through the restaurant. She wore a blue form-fitting dress with a sober but delicate décolletage: conservative, but extremely graceful. Sir Francis had expected a typical police officer and realized immediately that Victoria was much more than that. She was a woman, and she was strong.

At sixty and as a widower of five years, Sir Francis had developed a penchant for Chinese women and flirted with Victoria. She just watched him with her impenetrable eyes. After a while, she took out her Samsung phone to read her e-mails, completely disinterested in Sir Francis's compliments. She had experienced similar attempted seductions before.

When Sir Francis stopped talking, Victoria told him, "I have no interest in working for a firm run by a flirtatious British aristocrat. I like my job at the Hong Kong Police. Why should I join Pegasus? Is this how you treat women in your office?"

To say the least, Sir Francis had not expected such a direct response. However, he had immediately recognized that Victoria had one of the strongest qualities needed at Pegasus: a capacity to resist the unusual physical and emotional pressure detectives often found themselves under. Victoria would be a great recruit. Sir Francis had realized that, as many men did, he had mistaken her femininity for seduction. He needed to change his angle if he wanted to persuade her to join Pegasus.

Diana Yu had prepared Victoria for Sir Francis's flirtation, so Victoria held the advantage and had now ensured that she would be recruited for her professional merit even though she knew Sir Francis would probably remain attracted to her.

"I apologize for behaving as I did," Sir Francis said. "It will never happen again, and rest assured that harassment is not part of Pegasus's culture."

He stood up, left the table, and came back recomposed a few minutes later. "I am Francis Brian, and I gather you are Victoria Leung."

Victoria burst into laughter at Sir Francis's stiff upper lip and decided to give him a second chance.

"I'm not sure I know why I've agreed to meet you," Victoria teased. "A mutual friend, Henry Chu, told me you were looking for a senior detective. I thought this restaurant was good enough to justify spending a couple of hours with you, but don't expect me to be complacent."

Victoria didn't let on that she had been looking for new job opportunities and had thoroughly studied all the public information she could find on the secretive Pegasus firm, headquartered in a small Georgian house in the Park Place neighborhood of London, next to the St. James and Royal Overseas Clubs and the Ritz.

11

Victoria grabbed the *Southern China Morning Post*, Hong Kong's English newspaper, and read about the gay pride parade that had taken place the weekend before. Beijing didn't like it but felt they couldn't stop it. Plus, they had other fish to fry: they had decided to control the 2015 election of the Hong Kong Assembly, and the announcement had not been well received. While Beijing had permeated the administration and political leadership of the Special Administrative Region of Hong Kong, they were carefully focusing on its political functions and had a heavy hand on police and justice. That didn't extend to parades, but it did extend to demonstrations.

Victoria flipped to the *SCMP*'s economics section and saw an article by Feng Wang that included interviews of some of Bertrand Wilmington's colleagues who blamed the stress and the new regulations for his death. None of them alluded to a possible murder. She decided to call Feng.

"Hello. It's Victoria Leung here."

"Hello, Victoria. Good to hear your voice. How is life at Pegasus?"

"Different and unpredictable. I like it, even though I feel sometimes more exposed than I did when I was at the police. We're currently very busy."

"Be sure you remain well. You sometimes ask too much of yourself."

"I read your article in today's *SCMP*. Do you have more information about that death?"

"Are you asking about the investigation?"

"Which investigation is that?"

"BHS managed to get the police off their backs, but Harvey Lee, the general counsel, has begun an internal investigation."

Victoria was surprised by the news; Henry hadn't mentioned it. Could that be one of his reasons for hiring Pegasus? Could he be a target of the inquiry? That could explain his nervousness.

Feng continued. "They prefer not to air their dirty laundry in public, but banks aren't immune to bad publicity. There is consensus that there's more to the story than just a burned-out trader committing suicide. John Wilcox and Harvey Lee are adamant about it."

"How interesting. They certainly are discreet about it."

"So am I. I have some insights but nothing I would publish now."

"I thought your article today was interesting."

"What's your interest in this affair, if I may ask?"

"We have a client who also wants to get to the bottom of this death and feels uncomfortable with the police's superficial investigation and quick conclusion of suicide."

"Who is your client?"

Victoria smiled. "Feng, you know better than to ask that."

"Is your client within or outside BHS?"

"Within. I can't say more."

"What do you think at this stage?" Feng asked.

"Much too early to conclude, but the pieces of the puzzle I've managed to assemble so far suggest several possible scenarios and no clear direction. I wonder if BHS really wants to discover the truth."

"Oh yes. Harvey Lee is very upset by this situation, to put it mildly. He will get to the bottom of it. Whether *we* will learn the truth is not certain. Too many people have competing interests."

"That's what makes the case so complex and interesting for people like you and me. How is Nancy?"

"She just came back from Guangzhou; that city is moving fast. The old Cantonese blood is clearly active again, and they certainly are not short of initiatives, although their execution can be weak. It should become as attractive a city as Shanghai. Nancy loves her work as a liaison officer between the two cities. She's in Guangzhou once a month."

Even when she was with the police, Victoria and Feng sometimes discussed cases and compared notes, although they were careful to maintain each other's confidentiality. Their relationship had been helpful in the past and even decisive for some complex cases.

Before hanging up, Feng invited Victoria to dinner the next time Nancy was in Guangzhou. Seeing each other was easier now than it had been when Victoria had been with the police and it would be nice to catch up.

12

As she sipped green tea in her office, Victoria went over the events of the previous day and the disturbing elements that had emerged. She wanted to talk to Sir Francis, and she found him in the hallway outside his office.

"Hello, Miss Victoria. Anything new?"

"Actually, yes. Tell me when you have a moment."

"Give me fifteen minutes to settle and catch up with my e-mails and London, and then I'll be all yours."

Back in her office, a headline popped up on her computer screen: the *Financial Times* had picked up Feng Wang's story. John Wauters, one of the most respected and widely read columnists of the pink newspaper, asked a blunt question: "How many more deaths will we need before regulators and management seriously look at the problems that stress in investment banking creates?"

Wauters made a few interesting points. Several suicides had happened in London, but this was a worldwide phenomenon. He also compared the situation with the nonfinancial world, using the France Telecom suicides as an example, and to the case of German intern

Conrad Metz at Bank of America Merrill Lynch, who had had a seizure and died after seventy-two hours without sleep, which revealed practices close to slavery. Whatever management said, the culture of overwork was strongly engrained in the world of investment banking, as it was at law firms. Such companies did not consider sleep deprivation to be a mental health issue. Wauters ended his editorial by asking, "Are investment bankers particularly vulnerable to pressure, or do management at the banks put excessive pressure on their employees?"

Victoria was reflecting on this question as Sir Francis came in and sat down across from her. He liked talking to his colleagues in their offices, as this made conversations less formal.

"Do you know Feng Wang at the *SCMP?*" Victoria asked. "He was chief economist at JP Morgan. He's very independent. You might have seen his article on Bertrand Wilmington's suicide; it was picked up the *FT* today."

"What's his link to our case?"

"He interviewed BHS employees about Bertrand's suicide. They were pretty consistent in their descriptions about the pressure they felt he was under and the additional aggravation of new regulations."

"I'm not surprised. Problems like these have been going on for too long in banking."

"What I thought most important is that Harvey Lee has taken it upon himself to launch an internal investigation into the death."

"Stuart McMahon, their group general counsel, must have backed him. He's an American lawyer with a long career at the US Treasury. They must have serious reasons to launch such an inquiry."

"Do you believe that he suspects something other than suicide?"

"He probably does. These kinds of tragedies don't happen without reason, and, often enough, those reasons come from office culture. But, we shouldn't jump to any conclusion. You mentioned before that Bertrand was gay and that Diana thought that might have something to do with his death."

"That is indeed part of the investigation. How would you feel about calling Harvey?"

"We can't involve him without Henry Chang's agreement, and at this stage I would be reluctant to ask him for that permission. It might make him suspicious of our motives. You can certainly ask him, though."

"I suggested to Henry that I visit the BHS offices Monday evening to look at Bertrand's most recent trading activity. Maybe I should wait to hear from him."

"Can you access the data without going to the premises?"

"I doubt it. BHS has a reputation as an IT fortress, and their cyber-security has never been cracked. They rely on proprietary encryption. We could only retrieve the data by using Henry Chang's access. This, too, might expose him."

"One more reason to do everything above board."

Sir Francis left gracefully with a warm and supportive smile. Victoria responded in kind. There was something between them that would never be tested. They both knew it, and even if it wasn't always comfortable, it was their *modus operandi*.

Victoria decided to turn to the issue of Bertrand Wilmington's homosexuality. What Diana had told her was sufficiently graphic and explicit to warrant further investigation.

13

At fourteen, when he was camping in Maine, Bertrand took part in a night game organized by a few groups of boys along the river. Bertrand's two partners were two years older and led the quest to find out more about the mystery of the convent next to the camp. Bertrand didn't know them very well but he felt safe. The weather was hot, so they wore only shorts and T-shirts.

John Kirkpatrick was blond and tall. He spoke softly and with certain mannerisms that Bertrand wasn't apt to connect to homosexuality. Philip Smith was shorter and had dark hair but was clearly the leader of the team. He was part of his school's rowing team and had become a veritable star athlete.

At one stage, John and Philip held hands and kissed. Bertrand was surprised that they would act that way in front of him, and they asked him whether he had ever had sex with boys. He said he had not, and they came close and started undressing him. He tried to resist but couldn't escape. They took turns playing with him. They weren't rough. In fact, he felt warm under their touches and eventually enjoyed a pleasure he had never felt before. They made him swear never to disclose what had happened that night. Before then, he had only known solitary pleasure, a mortal sin according to the Catholic Church.

Bertrand later joined John and Philip's circle of friends and liberated his homosexuality. He learned how to caress and be caressed. By the time he joined his parents in Hong Kong to study at the University of Hong Kong, his sexual inclination was firmly established. He was sensitive and nice to women and sometimes enjoyed sleeping with them, but his passion was elsewhere.

Going back to the gay community and its networks was not a problem for Victoria Leung. Like many teenagers, when she was studying at Saint Mary's College in Singapore, an all-women's Catholic institution, she had developed a crush on one of her college professors. Victoria thought she was lesbian as a result.

As a junior, Victoria joined the swimming team, whose coach was a tall and very tough woman. Alexandra Wong had herself been seduced by one of her professors when she was thirteen. This was a turning point for Alexandra's sexual identity: she discovered she was a lesbian.

By her junior year, Victoria was a beautiful young woman, although still a bit of a tomboy. She had experienced some kissing and petting before she met Alexandra, but nothing particularly unconventional.

Bad news from her family shattered Victoria in the middle of that year, and Alexandra noticed during a training session that something was disturbing her. At the end of the session, Alexandra approached her.

"You seem disconnected, and I don't see your usual energy and discipline. Is something bothering you?"

"I have been distracted lately. My grandmother is in the hospital after a heart attack. Doctors are trying to diagnose exactly what can be done to treat her chronic heart disease, a condition that seems to stem from her youth. The conditions on the Mainland were sometimes precarious, and that's one of the reasons that my family moved to Hong

Kong and settled in Kowloon. She educated me, and I'm scared that she might die."

"I understand. Why didn't you tell me that earlier?"

"I'm a bit lost here and tend to keep my troubles to myself."

"That's not smart, Victoria. Nobody can survive thousands of miles away from home without emotional support. Please talk to me whenever you want. Are you familiar with Thai massage? I can always give you one. You'd be amazed how well it reduces tension." She hugged Victoria and kissed her on the forehead.

A week later, Alexandra proposed an hour-long massage after practice, and Victoria agreed. Alexandra's hands were strong and soft at the same time. Relief came quickly from Alexandra's intense work on her trouble spots and the warmth of her touch. Alexandra was truly an expert masseuse. Victoria then pushed her toward the most intimate parts of her body. That was the beginning of Victoria's bisexual life.

Victoria called Diana Yu and to ask if she knew how to reach Louis Cheung, Bertrand Wilmington's college friend. Diana gave her the information.

"I think he might be able to help me figure out whether the gay community has anything to do with Bertrand's death."

"You're probably right. I assume he knows. I met Louis only once, and he is such a delightful man; so sweet and charming."

"I wish you could join me, but that might get you in trouble."

The Hong Kong Police's code of conduct strictly prohibited joint interrogations with private detectives, like many police forces. In addition, any police involvement automatically became public record.

Louis lived in Kowloon. Victoria had developed her own inner strength during her difficult childhood in West Kowloon. Her parents had run a restaurant and had little time for her. Instead, her grand-mother educated her and gave her the affection that her parents could not. She had to fight to get where she was now, driven by a deep belief in equity.

Victoria called Louis on his mobile phone. "Good morning, Louis. My name is Victoria Leung. I work for Pegasus, a private British detective firm located in Hong Kong. I'm inquiring about Bertrand Wilmington's death and would very much like to meet you."

"Do I know you? Who gave you my phone number?"

"A mutual friend, Diana Yu."

"What do you want to know?"

"In the beginning of our investigation, your name came up as a close college friend of Bertrand Wilmington's. My client believes that there might have been more to his death has been explained."

"Bertrand would never have committed suicide unless he was pushed to do it, physically or emotionally. I am shocked, and I've wondered whether the police are covering up something at BHS by ruling it a suicide so quickly. So if you truly want to understand what happened to Bertrand, you can count me in. I also want to know what happened in that banking boiler room that might have pushed Bertrand to act that way."

He spoke with a mixture of anger and distress. The tragedy had affected him more than anybody Victoria had met so far.

"I live in Tsim Sha Tsui, like you," Victoria said. "Would it be possible for us to meet there for dinner?"

"I assume that sooner is better."

"Yes. Time is not our friend here. If there is any evidence, it will disappear very soon."

"Right. I'll meet you at the Macau restaurant on Nathan Road tonight at eight."

Victoria felt good about Louis Cheung's response. Initial informa-tion often gave a case its momentum. Louis seemed sincere about his willingness to help, and their one-on-one meeting might cut through the discretion—bordering on opacity—of the gay community.

Even if Louis didn't have any specific information, he probably was one of the few people who had known Bertrand Wilmington intimately and could share important information about his character. Victoria knew, too, that people reached out to close friends when in distress.

On that note, she prepared a jasmine green tea and searched for information about Louis Cheung's life, friends, adventures, and activities. Victoria was fastidious, and she had a genuine instinct for uncovering clues. She had a special talent for seeing stories in numbers that few financial specialists had. Victoria loved the hunt and was a skilled *chasseresse*.

14

IT WAS TUESDAY, AND PEGASUS DETECTIVES HAD THEIR WEEKLY meeting to discuss cases and share impressions and viewpoints. Victoria was looking forward to her colleagues' reactions to her investigation. When it came up, Sir Francis summarized the circumstances surrounding the case and asked Victoria to present the current status.

"At this stage, all of what I have been told so far leads me to believe that there is more to this case than meets the eye. Clearly, Bertrand Wilmington was in the middle of an intricate web that included homosexuality and suspicious trading practices and compliance at BHS. It's too early to say how the professional circumstances and personal dimensions combine, however. I am also uncertain of our client's motivations. Henry Chang might be trying to create his own defense with Pegasus's help. He hasn't been straightforward, and I'm almost certain that he's hiding his real agenda. If Bertrand Wilmington was murdered, Henry would be an obvious suspect."

Sir Francis was keen to have the team's input on this delicate matter.

"Does anybody have any information about our client Henry Chang?"

"I do," said Laura Woo, from the end of the table. She had worked part-time as a senior advisor to Pegasus since resigning as chair of the Hong Kong Securities and Futures Commission, better known as the SFC. Her counsel was precious because of her humanity as much as her experience and intelligence.

Laura's career spoke for itself. A lawyer of high academic credentials, including a three-year stint as a visiting professor at Columbia Law School and her current position teaching securities regulation at the University of Hong Kong Law School, Laura had been asked by the Chinese government to help structure governance practices at the CSRC in Beijing five years earlier. She had great integrity and had seen enough securities fraud to lose any illusions about the governance of investment banks. She had in-depth knowledge of both Hong Kong and Mainland securities regulation, the backbone of the Chinese markets since the end of British rule. Laura was universally renowned, and she regularly attended and spoke at the International Organization of Securities Commissions.

"I met him in the context of an investigation related to a securities fraud," Laura continued. "You might remember the flotation of the Oriental Real Estate. It was hugely oversubscribed, and allocations were seriously questioned. We launched an inquiry about the matter and, during the investigation, met senior executives of the lead managers of the transaction. At that time, Henry Chang was working at BHS's equity-capital-market desk, in charge of equity IPOs. For those who aren't as familiar as Victoria and I are with the banking world, the equity-capital-market desk is responsible for fixing the price of a new issue of shares, and it assumes the risk for the placement of the securities. If the issue is hot, the share price will increase, which in turn increases the benefits substantially. This is why the law prohibits firms from allocating shares to their employees, especially members of the equity teams.

"When Henry came to meet us, he was articulate and knowledgeable, and his facts were unquestionable. The evidence he provided us led to the dismissal of allegations of BHS's involvement in a scam, and proved very lucrative to some other firms. My only concern about him is that he can come across as too good to be true. But that doesn't tell you whether he's a hero or a villain."

"Does that mean we should be careful with him?" Victoria asked.

"I believe so, because he operates at multiple levels. He constantly jumps from the short term to the long term, from facts to opinions, and from personal to business interests. He's a golden boy and a moneymaker, but that doesn't make him an angel. We definitely need to investigate his assertions."

"Could he have an ulterior motive?"

"He probably does," Laura said. "Don't take his words at face value."

This was the first time Victoria had heard an assessment of Henry Chang as a professional. It confirmed her instinctive prudence. He would not be an easy client.

"I am grateful to you, Laura," Victoria said.

"At some stage, I might also want to reach out to BHS's general counsel, who launched an internal investigation," Sir Francis said. "We're lucky to have Harvey Lee in that position."

"Yes, indeed," Laura said. "He was a commissioner at the SFC when I was the chair. If he launched the internal inquiry, he must have serious reasons to believe that something suspicious is going on. It might be wider than the suicide case."

"When the time comes to reach out to BHS, we will certainly get you involved to be sure we are doing it right," Sir Francis said.

Victoria nodded. "In the meantime, I'll refresh my memory about BHS's relationship with the SFC."

As she left the meeting, Victoria was relieved not to be the only person questioning Henry Chang's motives. The web was getting thicker. She liked this kind of challenge.

"Do you have a second for me?" Sir Francis asked.

"With pleasure."

They went to his office, which was decorated with an exquisite mix of English mahogany and modern furniture and contemporary Chinese artwork that lent peace to the room and promoted confidence.

"I thought Laura was especially insightful," Sir Francis said. "It will be helpful to get information from her personal connections there about what the SFC has pending with BHS."

Victoria agreed. "On another note, I thought of inviting Diana Yu for dinner. The fact that she was Henry Chang's intermediary surprised me after what happened between them. How do you feel about it?"

"I see no reason why you shouldn't see her as a friend, but I wouldn't recommend that you bring up this investigation. Let her take the initiative. After all, I wouldn't want her to interpret the dinner as a quest for information. Keep me posted."

15

VICTORIA SPENT THE AFTERNOON GATHERING ALL THE BACK-ground information she could find on the actors currently central to the case.

Her search landed on some new information about Louis Cheung: he had been born and raised in Macau, a former Portuguese colony reunited with China in 1999 that was now the Las Vegas of China. He had attended Harrow International School, the first boarding school created by the British government for the children of their representatives in Hong Kong.

Unlike Bertrand, Louis hadn't stayed long at BHS. After only a couple of years at the firm's hedge fund, he started a hospitality career at the Mandarin Oriental and had foreign assignments in London, Singapore, and New York. His father wanted him to have the best training before taking the reins of a luxury hotel. He himself had been in charge of food and beverage at a luxury Macau hotel, so he knew that the hospitality industry was a tough one populated by too many amateurs.

Louis had chosen the Macau restaurant in Tsim Sha Tsui because of his familiarity with the area. It wasn't a fancy restaurant, but it was convenient for both of them.

Louis was already sitting at a corner table when Victoria arrived. He seemed at home; he was engaged with a waiter in a lively conversation about the Australian Open tennis championship. Maybe Louis's father owned the place, Victoria speculated. Fewer business people were here than would be at a regular hotel restaurant. Victoria was looking forward to the meal as she had no doubt about the freshness of the seafood, the staple of Macau cuisine.

"Good evening, Victoria. Great to see you. Do you know this place?"

"I live around the corner and walk by it almost every day, but I've never eaten here. I generally cook at home."

They chatted about life in Kowloon and business in Hong Kong, and they shared the common complaints about the difficulties of getting around. Louis ordered a series of Macau specialties for them to sample.

"So, Bertrand," he said with a sigh.

"Yes, Bertrand," Victoria said. "It must have been a terrible loss for you."

"I cannot believe he is no longer here. When I worked abroad for Mandarin Oriental, we met less frequently, but each time we did, it was as if we had never left university. When I came back here, we both had hectic calendars, and it was almost a miracle to find an evening, let alone a day, to be together."

Louis had spoken quietly, but his anger at Bertrand's death was evident. He remained silent for a few long moments, evidently attempting to compose himself. His anger was palpable.

"How did you guys meet?" Victoria asked.

"We took gymnastics classes and participated in competitions together. He was so talented. We had a natural affinity for each other, having both attended British boarding schools. The sad thing is that we had to hide our relationship."

The truth came out quickly. Louis seemed comfortable with Victoria.

"When you met him recently, did he seem tense or worried?"

"He did indeed. He had received e-mails from a senior guy at BHS threatening to publicize our relationship if we didn't join him to 'have fun,' as he put it."

"Who was the sender?"

"The head of their back office."

"How did Bertrand react?"

"He was upset but had to hide it at work. He had apparently talked about it with a senior person. I don't remember the name. A lawyer."

"Could it have been Harvey Lee?"

"No, it was a woman."

"Could you describe Bertrand to me, if it's not asking too much?"

"Of course. As I told you, if anybody is responsible for Bertrand's death, I will do anything I can to make sure he or she gets arrested. Bertrand was a good and caring man. It was initially difficult for his parents to accept that he was gay and that we were in a relationship. He had been passionate about financial innovation and thought derivatives were the best thing since sliced bread, but that passion had faded recently."

"Was it because of the e-mails?"

"No, he had already had enough six months ago. It seems it was very hard to be gay in a huge trading room. He wanted to leave. He tried to explain the conditions to me, but I couldn't understand. He was ethical and believed in regulation, Chinese walls, and all that stuff."

They both laughed at the expression the Chinese used for barriers erected in businesses to prevent conflicts of interests even though it had origins in the Great Wall of China.

The waiters loaded the table with the dishes Louis had ordered, and Louis explained the ingredients in each one and how the dish was cooked. Victoria was glad to see so much seafood and vegetables, and she knew the meal would be light and tasty. Macanese cuisine, not as well-known as its Chinese counterparts, had similar flavors to Mediterranean food.

"Would the circumstances at the office be enough to lead Bertrand to commit suicide?" Victoria asked.

"It would highly surprise me. He mentioned harassment as an annoyance in trading rooms, but it happens most often to assistant traders, who are mostly young women, some of whom dream of marrying traders."

"I was in the audit department of CITIC and encountered my fair share of it. There is very little one can do. Either you bear it or you leave. After one too many instances, I left. I went to the financial fraud office of the Hong Kong Police."

"That is brave of you. It really takes guts to do that. Your paycheck must have suffered substantially."

"Yes. Even though the financial fraud department is slightly better paid than others, my monthly take-home was less than half of what I got at CITIC."

"You are a very intelligent woman. There was no reason to put up with that behavior."

"The combination of power, sex, and money disturbed me. In an audit function, the front office has so much power and brings in so much money that it's very rare for management to rule in favor of integrity. They can't afford to lose the money machines upstairs."

"Bertrand thought he had found something irregular that compromised him and the firm. He was about to act on it."

"Was it about sexual harassment?"

"No, he didn't believe that BHS would listen to complaints of sexual harassment. When he talked about it, he said he needed more evidence about the exact transactions and how much money was involved."

"How would he have found out about it?"

"He had befriended Olivia Schuler, David Chen's secretary. She's a nice Swiss woman whose husband works at the UNICEF office in Hong Kong and who actively supports children on the Mainland."

"How did they meet?"

"Bertrand met her at a reception at the Swiss Embassy. She was disturbed by some of her boss's behavior. Please keep this to yourself. I don't want Olivia to suffer because of it. She told Bertrand she was willing to come forward once his investigation had closed."

"Did you meet her?"

"Yes, she was at a party at my hotel, and Bertrand introduced her to me. She is really trustworthy. She must be shattered now. They became close and supported each other. Bertrand was really fond of her. She was courageous and didn't hesitate to confront her temperamental boss when he went too far."

"Can I contact her?"

"Please don't. Since BHS has started an inquiry, it would be better to ensure that they interview her. If she speaks to you, she'll probably feel that she's betraying her employer and, more dangerously, her boss."

"You may be right."

Victoria was touched by Louis's kindness, despite his grief. The way he protected Olivia Shuler was, at the same time, firm and sensitive. He exuded warmth. He must have been a wonderful partner for Bertrand Wilmington.

16

AT THAT MOMENT, THREE WESTERN LOOKING MEN STORMED INTO the restaurant yelling profanity and offensive slurs. They looked drugged or drunk. The restaurateur immediately called the police.

The men, dressed in black, looked the clients over, as if searching for a victim. They approached Louis Cheung.

"Look who it is, our chicken, Louis," said one of the men, a blond guy with a strong accent. "You remember the University of Hong Kong? Weren't you with the guy who died at BHS?"

"Yes," said a second man. "And with a lady on top of that. She must be queer. They must be great in bed together."

"Get up, Louis," the first man said. "We want to talk to you outside. Bring the lady too. We might have fun with her."

They tried to pull Victoria and Louis up from their table, but they didn't move.

"Get up or someone is going to get hurt!" the gang members yelled.

The blond guy, who seemed to be the leader, grabbed Louis by the arm and squeezed hard. Louis cried out in pain but tried to protect Victoria. An elderly couple stood up and intervened, giving the restaurant manager time to grab the second man by his collar, destabilizing him. Another customer intervened and even pulled the second man's hair.

During the struggle, Victoria fled outside and collapsed on the pavement. But before she could react, the leader of the group ran out after her and dragged her back inside. He tore off her shirt and bra, bruising her. His nails were scratching her deeply and she felt the warmth of blood. His body was heavy on top of her and he was attempting to force himself inside of her, but somehow, Victoria managed to push him off, knee him hard in the groin and get to her feet.

Victoria regained her full control and used her martial arts training to aggressively push her attacker as far away as she could. He screamed in pain but went silent when a large pan hit him on the head. Victoria dragged the gang leader by the collar and waistband, and ran toward Louis, who could hardly resist the other two assailants. Throwing the leader to the side, Victoria knocked them down in a single stroke.

Sounds of police sirens approached, and the three men scattered just before three officers entered the restaurant.

A second car arrived, and two female officers attended to Victoria, whose skirt and shirt had been stained with blood. The officers led her to the bathroom, and she managed to put herself in order, but she shook with the shock. Back in the restaurant, an officer gave her a blanket.

An emergency team put Louis in an ambulance, and Victoria went to him. He was in bad shape: his face had been seriously bruised in the brutal beating, and cuts appeared on his body. His left arm was bandaged.

"How bad is it?" Victoria asked. She took his hand and saw tears in his eyes. They both sobbed.

"Pretty bad. My left arm is probably broken. They gave me painkillers. I probably have a concussion. What about you?"

"One of them tried to rape me, but I stopped him and the manager hit him on the head with a pan. My wounds should be superficial."

"I see lots of blood ..."

"I have never seen such hatred," Victoria said. "Please take care of yourself. Should I call somebody for you?"

"No, I already called my parents. My brother is on his way to the hospital." Louis apologized for having gotten her involved in the attack. He then said he would send her an e-mail with the name of one of the aggressors, whom he recognized.

When the ambulance left, the senior female officer asked Victoria what had happened. Victoria gave her a short version of the story, blaming drinking and drugs more than homophobia. She didn't want to complicate Louis's life after the ordeal he had been through.

When Victoria gave her name, the officer asked, "Didn't you work at police headquarters? I recognize your name. You won an award for the Sun Hung Kai scandal. The Flying Dragon, no?"

"Yes, that was a special case."

"You had a big influence on my decision to join the force. Is there anything I can do for you?"

"Yes. I would like to know more about what those attackers were up to. Please let me know what you find out."

"I definitely will."

The officer insisted that Victoria go to the hospital, but she preferred her apartment. The two officers drove Victoria home and accompanied her inside to ensure that she was able to be alone.

"Do you remember any of those guys?" a policeman asked Louis in the ambulance.

"Yes, I do. The tall guy, the leader of the group, was a well-known bully at the University of Hong Kong and the star of the cricket team. I reported his actions, but to no avail. You know how it is at many universities; sports and athletics sometimes overshadow harassment. It happens at everywhere, even in the United States and Britain."

"Please send me their names if you have them."

"I will."

As she removed her clothes in the bathroom, Victoria examined the effects of her aggressors' violence. She had bruises on her chest and between her legs, which she could hide, but also one on her forehead. She took a photo of the wounds in case someone would investigate. Professional reflex. She applied first aid. There were no signs of internal harm or any broken bones.

She took a hot bath, even though it hurt. She needed to wash off any trace of the man who assaulted her. She made an exception to her rules and sipped a glass of an Old Portuguese Port from San Martinho do Porto. As her mind raced with questions about sexuality, crime, violence, and rape, a text from Louis came in: "The name of the assailant is Wieslaw Mysliwski."

Victoria smiled. A Polish fascist?

Another text came in: "I found him on LinkedIn. He started working at Bank Handlowy w Warzawe in Warsaw. Traveled to London for them and was recruited after University of Hong Kong by ... BHS. He's a trader in the fixed-income department."

"Thank you," she answered. "This can't be a coincidence. Is your arm broken?"

"Yes. I'm in a temporary cast. Take care of yourself. I know how much it hurts. Violence is unbearable. I hate it and am so ashamed of the way some men can behave."

"Don't be ashamed. You're not one of them. Good night, Louis."

Louis's message was so sweet. It was this kind of compassion that made humankind so precious. She put on a robe and went to the bedroom, her eyes welling with the warm tears that cleaned the soul. She took painkillers and crashed on the bed. She managed to get some sleep, but her night was tormented.

It was not the first time that she had been a victim of harassment and violence, but this was the first sexual assault she had endured.

17

HONG KONG WAS KNOWN FOR ITS WEAK LAWS AGAINST RAPE. Victoria knew too well that the police—not to mention the media—often turned victims into suspects, so few rape cases were actually reported to anyone other than social workers. Fortunately, Victoria managed to fight off her attacker. She could have sustained far more debilitating trauma and injury.

To make things worse, Secretary of Security Lai Tung-Kwok appeared at a Fight Crime Committee meeting to discuss the soaring rape statistics reported in the *Standard*. Instead of pointing the finger at the true culprits, Lai suggested that women's drinking habits might be to blame.

Women at the police force hotly debated the issue. They were shocked by the behavior of some of their male colleagues and had recently managed to create a special force comprised of policewomen, psychologists, and doctors. These women knew the dangers they faced at crime scenes and in the office and that such threats were common in other traditionally male-dominated institutions.

Victoria dressed in pants and a turtleneck to hide her bruises at the office, and she hoped nobody would pay much attention to her forehead.

As she sipped her green tea at her desk, Sir Francis popped in. She didn't want to talk to him. Men could react strangely when informed of sexual violence.

He pointed to the bruise on her forehead. "Did you hurt yourself?"

"Yes. It's nothing serious. Thank you for asking."

"Are you sure? Have you seen a doctor?"

"I don't believe I need to. I might if it gets worse."

Sir Francis dropped the subject and left, but Victoria knew he didn't believe her. His British education had taught him to be excessively discreet, but he had learned to be vigilant without putting pressure on a subject. This was always a concern when working with young female detectives. Sometimes he was patronizing, but he believed that was preferable to being lax.

Victoria was still thinking about the previous night when her colleague and friend Christine Freed came in. Christine had been key to Victoria joining Pegasus, and she was probably the only colleague Victoria could trust in such a tough situation. She was Australian and had come to Hong Kong with her fiancé, who quickly cheated on her with a Chinese girl. She had been in Hong Kong for five years now.

Judy Wang walked in as Victoria and Christine started talking. She immediately noticed the wound on Victoria's forehead.

"Who hit you?"

Victoria was surprised. *Was the bruise that obvious?* "I hurt myself last night."

"Don't give me that nonsense, Victoria. Somebody hit you. Did you have a fight?" She half smiled.

"Yes," added Christine. "You can't fool us. What happened to you?" She delicately touched the bruise. "A bruise like that doesn't come from hurting yourself, Vic. And it's swollen. What happened to you?"

"I told you. I hurt myself." Like many other Chinese women,

Victoria acted defensively to hide her pain. She couldn't bear the stigma of having been sexually assaulted.

"Was it that brutal?"

"What do you mean?"

"You're still in shock, and you turned your eyes away from me when I asked you if you had been hit. It's not like you, Vic. If it was something minor, you would have admitted it. Have you been assaulted?"

Victoria nodded. Tears rolled down her cheeks, and she sobbed. Christine held her in her arms without a word, and Judy fetched tea, a towel, and hot water. It took several long minutes before Victoria managed to compose herself.

She then told Christine and Judy, who never interrupted her, what happened the previous night. It was a long and painful account.

At the end, Christine asked quietly, "Do you intend to talk about it with Sir Francis?"

"I don't want to."

"Look, this was life threatening, and if it hadn't been for the old couple and the restaurateur, God knows where you would be today. Furthermore, it may be related to your investigation. Sir Francis should know."

"I don't want to tell him. He is my boss."

"Will you report it to the police?"

"I won't have to since the police were on the crime scene very quickly." Victoria said, raising her voice. "I would advise any woman to report something like this. We need to lock up those bastards. They use sex as a weapon, and they know women can't always physically resist them. I want to make this an example of the misconduct of men and homophobia. I hate those monsters."

All her body tensed, ready for a fight. It was the first time she was able to vent her outrage at this plague on society. She looked out the window and took a few minutes to calm down. *Why did she have to be a victim?* "How could those men have been so bestial?" Victoria yelled. "I'm sorry."

"Don't be sorry, or you'll infuriate us," Christine said. "You are perfectly sane and entitled to that anger."

"I refuse the public stigma of being a raped woman. It's hard enough to have endured the attack. I won't let men's despicable actions define me. I will testify if they're eventually brought to trial."

"Would you like us to talk to Sir Francis together?" Christine said. "I can tell him what happened in a careful way. We need direction on this. This is now integral part of your investigation and the firm's responsibility."

Victoria liked Christine's proposal and agreed. They finished their tea, the silence saying so much more than words could. Victoria used the moment of meditation to prepare for the difficult next step.

She then looked her colleagues in the eye and nodded. "Thank you. Give me a moment."

They all smiled at each other. The women's hugs comforted Victoria. Some important healing was beginning.

18

"Harvey, I thought I would call you personally," Hong Kong Police Commissioner Liu Chu said over the phone.

Throughout his years as general counsel of BHS, Harvey had probably spoken to Liu Chu half a dozen times. "It must be a serious matter, Commissioner. Tell me what it's about."

"Last night, a trio of antigay activists went to a restaurant and attacked two diners, a man and a woman. The attackers apparently knew the man from college and beat him extensively. They also tried to rape the woman."

"That is really serious. How does that involve my bank or me?"

"The leader of the trio, Wieslaw Mysliwski, is an employee of your bank. He works in the fixed-income department. He and his accomplices are in custody."

During the long silence that followed, Harvey processed this information. He had been informed of antigay activities in the fixed-income department. Some employees even speculated that homosexuality might have somehow played a role in Bertrand Wilmington's death. But the antigay segment had resisted management's attempts to eradicate it.

"Could we keep this discreet?" Harvey asked.

"Yes, but not for more than two or three days. You know how things go."

"I need those days. I have myself launched an internal inquiry into some practices in this department, and Wieslaw Mysliwski is on the list of the people I need to talk to. I assume you intend to interrogate him?"

"I will. We won't disclose it in order to prevent leaks to the media. I'll call you if anything changes. That should give you enough time to get more information."

"This could be very bad. You can be sure that I'm handling the matter personally. I'll keep you informed."

Harvey hung up and paced in his office. It was the best way for him to concentrate and alleviate the stress.

This wasn't the first time he had been confronted with issues from the trading rooms, which were like high schools with their cliques and bullies. Traders were more often recruited for their aggressiveness than for their maturity and respect for the rules. Banks rarely put them under a leadership that could deal with this culture. Instead, most leaders emerged from the traders' ranks and acted just like them.

Harvey decided to handle the matter in a way that wouldn't involve anybody from outside of his department. He thought it fortunate that nobody was focusing on the connection to Bertrand Wilmington's death since the police had concluded it a suicide. Harvey was far from certain of that conclusion.

This new assault made his life more difficult, though. With only three days to investigate, he needed to instill a sense of urgency in everybody involved in the inquiry.

Commissioner Chu had put the conversation with Harvey Lee on speaker phone so his deputy could listen.

"You're taking risks, Commissioner Chu. What if BHS finds nothing?"

"I know," Chu said quietly, "but I also know Harvey very well. We studied law together in the UK. He wouldn't want me to wait unless he was sure something very serious was going on. In any event, I can always interrupt the truce."

"Could this have anything to do with the suicide at BHS? I thought the victim was also a homosexual man in the trading room."

"I doubt it, but we should look at every incident involving BHS from the past twelve months. You never know. Let's put the fraud department on the case as well."

"That reassures me. I'll ask Diana Yu to look at the files."

───────────────

When Diana Yu got the assignment from the deputy commissioner, her heart raced. She had been shocked by the police's rapid ruling of suicide in Bertrand Wilmington's case, and this brought her situation with Henry Chang to the forefront.

As always, Diana's bosses didn't give her any hint about the reason for the demand. The deputy commissioner had simply said, "I believe that you know banking activities and could be of help here."

That was as much of a recognition of her competence and value as she had ever received from a superior since she had joined the police force. Something serious must have happened.

Diana immediately went to her computer to search the files. The first incidents she found were meaningless: credit card fraud, loan recovery schemes, and some attempts to attack the branches.

But then a mention of Henry Chang in a report from the Hong Kong SFC surprised her. It was highly unusual for regulators to send a report to the police, and this indicated there was a serious suspicion of fraud.

The report related to speculation on the IPO of Oriental Real

Estate that was managed by BHS with a syndicate of powerful local and foreign investment banks. The equity-capital-market division, which managed the transaction, was suspected of manipulating the market to raise the price during the first week after the offering. The stock was ten times oversubscribed.

19

VICTORIA WENT WITH CHRISTINE TO SIR FRANCIS'S OFFICE. SHE recognized that she had no choice but to inform him, although she would have preferred to keep the matter private. Already in Sir Francis's office, Laura Woo stood up to leave, but Sir Francis asked her to stay.

Christine and Victoria were his two most senior female detectives and had sometimes been vocal about women's issues. He seemed to expect this meeting to be about that.

"Victoria was sexually assaulted during a dinner last night with Louis Cheung, the partner of Bertrand Wilmington," Christine said somberly.

"What happened?" Laura asked.

"This is a very delicate issue, and Victoria asked me to join her to inform you," Christine continued, directing the conversation at Sir Francis. "We need to work together on this. It has professional as well as personal ramifications for us."

Christine's firm but calm tone got Sir Francis's undivided attention. Victoria told Sir Francis what happened, without entering into unnecessary details.

Sir Francis didn't need to be persuaded to do something about this; he had encountered problems like this before and had been sensitive to them. However, he was so intensely affected by this particular incident that it was difficult for him to be involved. This would be the first time he would have to tackle it directly.

Sir Francis was clearly impressed by his detectives' approach. If this were the UK, the firm would make sure that Scotland Yard properly handled the victim, but here in Hong Kong, things weren't so simple. He took time to reflect before saying, "I perfectly understand where you're coming from, Victoria. You have immense sympathy from me on this, and I will do anything to support any course of action you decide to take."

He paused again and looked at his partners. He explained that he couldn't understand why men continued to assault women. The idea was totally contrary to his values. He worried that this plague would never be eradicated, but he would do anything he could to protect the victims and make sure the aggressors were brought to justice.

A deeply emotional silence followed. Victoria knew she would benefit from all the medical, psychological, and legal help that the firm could offer, but she still had to deal with the brutality of the crime she had endured. As she sat on the sofa, she put her head in her hands to hide her pain.

After a moment, she looked up again; she was not a wounded bird but an attacked adult. "Thank you, Francis and Laura," Victoria said assertively. "This means a lot to me. You and Christine know how involved I am in fighting violence against women. As a former member of the police force, the publicity I could endure might be difficult, though. The label rape victims receive and the stigma associated with it are sometimes worse than the attack itself."

Victoria's thoughts turned to the wider investigation. She was increasingly uneasy with limiting Pegasus's role only to what Henry Chang had requested. Too many aspects of the case now went beyond his personal interest.

"You know that I'll be meeting with Henry Chang tomorrow

to give him a progress report. I would like to extend our investigation beyond his interest. I'm unable to define where he is on all this, and he might be manipulating us. I'd prefer not to share everything with him."

"Would it help you to successfully conclude the investigation if you did that?" Sir Francis asked.

"Enormously, although I'd also like you to talk to Harvey Lee. I have no idea how BHS is looking at this case, and now their employee attacked Louis Cheung. I really need to look at this case in a holistic way."

"I will do it," Sir Francis said.

As the women left the office, Laura took Victoria's arm.

"Will you see a doctor? You need to be examined because you never know. At some point, you might need the evidence collected by a physician, and this isn't possible after twenty-four hours. If you want our health care coverage to treat consequences of this assault, you unfortunately need some medical attention."

"I will go and see my gynecologist. Would that be enough?"

"Absolutely," Laura said. "You can share the results with me if you'd like."

Victoria and Laura went to the Starbucks downstairs. At this moment, jasmine tea was not enough. Victoria needed a strong coffee.

20

Sir Francis called Harvey Lee to inform him of Pegasus's investigation into the death of Bertrand Wilmington. They met at the Hong Kong Club, which was particularly well equipped for discreet and friendly meetings. It had the atmosphere of a British club, including a smoking room for the two cigar aficionados. After the usual small talk, Sir Francis explained the situation.

"We're investigating the death of Bertrand Wilmington. At this stage, we wonder whether professional and personal elements might explain why he took his life."

"What elements?"

"Some antigay harassment and some suspicious trading practices occurred at BHS a few days before Bertrand died. And there may be other issues outside of your firm."

"How do you think these are related?"

"Some of the trades affected Bertrand's activities, and he might have been the subject of the harassment. Our client seems credible enough for us to accept that the police's ruling of suicide may be incorrect."

A waiter delivered the lamb chops and French beans they had ordered, giving Harvey time to decide whether he could trust Sir Francis with the details of his own investigation. Bringing him to the other side of the Chinese wall could have serious implications. He discussed the public angle first.

"Have you heard about the assault at the Macau restaurant last night?" Asked Harvey.

"Yes."

"One of our employees was one of the attackers. He works in the fixed-income department, as Bertrand did. The police commissioner has given me three days to find out more about him before they go public with this information."

"I knew that one of your former employees was involved."

"How?"

"There was more than one victim. The second was a woman, who was sexually assaulted. I know her personally."

"Do the police know that?"

"I don't know what the police know."

"That means that another victim might come forward. It doesn't leave us much time to get to the core of this despicable situation."

"That is indeed the risk. This is where I need your help. One of our senior detectives needs to have access to the trading data from the days prior to Bertrand's death. Could you allow her to look at it with your people after the market is closed this evening?"

He was clearly tempted to refuse the outside involvement. "I don't think your detective will understand our business."

"She will. She worked on the audit staff of CITIC's fixed-income department until a few years ago. Her name is Victoria Leung. She also spent a few years in the Hong Kong Police's fraud department."

"Victoria Leung . . . wasn't she the head of the task force that prompted the arrest of the two Kwok brothers in the Sun Hung Kai properties fraud? The Flying Dragon?"

"Yes."

"I saw her at meetings during that inquiry. She ran circles around us old, experienced male executives and lawyers. Granted, we were also mystified by her beauty and charm. Her combination of leadership, analytical skills, and intuition was very impressive. Getting that arrest was not easy."

"We should never underestimate the strength and obstinacy of Chinese women. Their juvenile looks sometimes hide character and strength. Crossing them is often a major mistake."

As they left the club, Harvey indicated that he would involve his audit and compliance colleagues and set a meeting at BHS headquarters for six that evening. Victoria should ask for him. Sir Francis was happy to have had that conversation. He planned to keep it quiet that the Flying Dragon and the female victim of the assault were the same person.

Harvey returned to his office impressed with Sir Francis's ability to connect the dots of complex elements of intelligence. He now had to elucidate the internal connections between the Macau restaurant incident, the Bertrand Wilmington suicide, and BHS's fixed-income trading all in only seventy-two hours. He would undoubtedly have little time to sleep and no margin for error.

Sir Francis immediately briefed Victoria and asked her if she felt capable of going to the meeting that evening. Victoria agreed. She was ready to look more closely at the dark side of the trading rooms. She was strongly convinced that she would find something relevant, and she enjoyed the opportunity to put her audit skills back in action.

Victoria called in a couple of junior detectives to provide her with everything they could find about BHS's trading operations and systems to prepare for the meeting.

21

Victoria's cell phone rang. She saw it was Diana Yu and picked up.

"Hello, Victoria. How have you been?"

"It's been tough, but nothing we should talk about on the phone. What are you up to?"

"I'm working on something close to what you're doing. Would you have time to meet? We could go to the Antique Patisserie. Their afternoon tea is exceptional."

"I can do that. Let's meet at four."

"That's perfect. See you there."

Victoria thought about how wide this case had become. Since last night, information was developing on all fronts, Victoria's personal involvement in the investigation was increasingly challenging, and now Diana wanted to meet where they could talk in confidence.

The Antique Patisserie had the look of something out of an English fairy tale and the best English tea in the city. It was also situated in the busiest area of Hong Kong: decades-old electric trams, small streets, completely hectic traffic, and the crowd of offices and shops made the district a good place to hang out and enjoy the buzz of the city.

"English tea for two?" a waitress asked when the friends sat down.

"We will share one afternoon tea with two cups," Diana answered.
"Would Earl Grey work for you, Victoria?"

"Indeed."

Diana seemed to notice Victoria's bruise but didn't mention it.
She knew her friend well enough to let her bring it up first.

"The Police Commissioner has asked me to investigate the activities of BHS, particularly possible problems in their fixed-income trading department. I don't believe in coincidences."

"I understand," Victoria said quietly. "What brought that about?"

"They wouldn't tell me, but I have forty-eight hours to come up with a full report. Since this came from Commissioner Chu and involves BHS, I was wondering whether it would have anything to do with what Henry Chang has asked you to investigate."

"I'm not sure," Victoria replied, "but I also find the coincidence troubling. I thought the police were sticking with the suicide ruling. This must mean that new elements have prompted the commissioner to reopen the case. That's highly unusual."

"I also heard that a gang of three antigay bullies attacked a man and a woman in Kowloon. One of those bullies is a trader at BHS. That might be the cause of this renewed interest in the bank."

"That might be connected with your inquiry. Do you think the commissioner has connected those dots?"

"Possibly," Diana answered. "How are things evolving in your inquiry?"

"We're not excluding anything, but I must confess that there are very few leads on the precise cause of Bertrand Wilmington's death. I still have my doubts about Henry, though."

"What happened to you?" Diana pointed to the bruise.

"I hit myself badly."

Victoria was not prepared to say more about the Macau restaurant events. Luckily, Diana didn't seem to have made the connection. The last thing she wanted was to have the police step in and interrogate her. She was lucky to have three days to work on her own without police interference. After that, the whole thing would go public. She needed to solve this case before that happened.

"Have you met with Henry recently?" Diana asked.

"I have an appointment with him tomorrow for a progress report. We haven't been in touch since he came to see me at the beginning of the investigation. Have you heard anything?"

"He seems to have flown to Bali to see his fiancée shoot her movie. I don't know if he's back."

"Well, he should be back by tomorrow."

"Don't trust him too much, Victoria. I'm not sure what's driving him. I don't see what's at stake here."

"Perhaps I'll know more tomorrow," Victoria replied.

What was Diana trying to tell her? The fact that she was investigating BHS? The urgency Commissioner Chu added to the case? The fact that Henry wasn't credible? All of these things raised warnings. The police were getting closer to BHS's fixed-income activities as a result of the attack. That was probably why the police commissioner had called Harvey Lee. If the picture wasn't clear, at least the players were all in motion.

Dr. Ng was an experienced gynecologist who kept a very human dimension to her practice. She had been Victoria's doctor for more than ten years, and Victoria trusted her completely. Dr. Ng knew more about Victoria's medical history than anybody else, and it was comforting that Dr. Ng always put Victoria's examination into the context of her whole life.

Dr. Ng's office was also welcoming, with photographs on the walls from her travels in Tibet. The landscape and the women in them made them so intimately present. The doctor welcomed Victoria with her usual warm smile.

"What happened, Victoria? You rarely come to me with an

emergency. This must be something serious. Or have you suddenly become pregnant?"

This was their usual inside joke. Dr. Ng was attentive to Victoria's fertility as it waned. They both laughed.

"Not yet," Victoria replied. Her tone became serious. "I was attacked last night by a group of antigay bullies. They thought I was gay because I was at dinner with a gay man. If an old couple hadn't rescued us, it would have been a lot worse. Could you examine me?"

Victoria shared the details of the assault with Dr. Ng.

"Before I do this, tell me how you feel emotionally," asked Dr. Ng.

"Like a woman who has been brutalized. I am really angry and hurt. The physical impact is bad enough, but the feeling of being a victim just because I'm a woman is unbearable. Yet, my injuries are mild compared to many other cases."

Dr. Ng explained that she was used to receiving emergency calls from women who had been assaulted or raped, and each call rallied her anger. Yet she knew that most of her clients would not risk going to the police. She had set up a support group for such women and referred some of her patients to it. Emotional distress was at least as important as the physical effects of rape.

She examined Victoria with great care and told her she could pick up the medical report if she didn't want to risk having it e-mailed.

"There are no internal problems, at least," Dr. Ng said. "Your injuries will heal within a couple of weeks, but do not underestimate the emotional shock. Come back in two weeks so I can assess your progress. In the meantime, I advise you to take some Chinese medicine to reduce your stress without sapping your energy."

They worked on the details, and Victoria left the office reassured. Laura Woo had been right to advise her to get examined.

22

WHEN VICTORIA RETURNED TO HER OFFICE, SHE ASKED THE RE-
search team to go over their findings with her. They had found little
evidence, but some social media messages were descriptive about the
amount of pressure traders at BHS faced. And they weren't the only
ones who faced it: employees of their competitors also said their managers were treating them like slaves, making it impossible to have lives
outside the office. That wasn't news; Feng Wang had documented it in
the *South China Morning Post*.

A post on a trader's social media site, the Tempest, caught
Victoria's attention. It was a favorite site among derivatives traders,
and a "Bertrand W." had posted a fairly dramatic message:

> *The new regulations are going to kill us. We cannot oper-*
> *ate in our market without confidentiality, but they want*
> *transparency. We will have a bloodbath in the industry.*
> *Some people are trying to capture maximum benefits*
> *from this interim period. Once the new regulations are*
> *in place, we will never see the level of activity that we're*
> *used to.*

He got a response from a colleague, Linda:

Adding sexual harassment for the juniors, it is terrible. I put up with it for three years. I am checking out. Life is too important. Get out, Bertrand, before it's too late. If they want to get you, they will. They can crush you. You are one of the few decent guys there. The bullies rule the place. And they have a coterie with their counterparts in other firms. Leave quickly before it's too late.

Bertrand W. did not answer this post until a week before he died, when he responded:

You are better than most of us. I decided to follow your advice. I hope it's not too late. I believe they're on to me now. I don't know if I can still escape. I am scared to death, Linda.

An hour later, Linda answered:

Get out if you still can. You cannot win that battle. There is no escape.

The day before his death, Bertrand replied:

You're right. I bought a ticket to Sydney.

That was certainly the clearest indication of Bertrand's fears. What was he going to do in Sydney?

It was time for Victoria to go to BHS headquarters and look into the trading.

The BHS building was very different from those built in the past twenty years that made the Hong Kong skyline so impressive. At night, the reflection in Kowloon Bay of its metal-and-glass expressionist façade left a unique impression. It was completed in 1985 after two years under construction. It dwarfed the English-style Old City Hall.

The foyer was stunning: several floors of open office spaces looked out onto a gigantic atrium that left visitors feeling like they had entered a modern cathedral. Whether one liked modern architecture or not, its power was astonishing.

Victoria felt this power; she really liked the design. The sunset glowed through the entire building. She marveled at its combination of grandiosity and lightness, at the classicism in what was not otherwise a classical construction.

Victoria was lost in her thoughts when a young security officer asked what she wanted. This gentle reminder that the bank expected its visitors to come for a purpose brought her back to her appointment with Harvey Lee. The officer directed her to a discreet desk and then to special elevators taking those who were authorized to visit the executive floors.

This would be hard business.

Victoria recognized Harvey Lee right away. She was struck by not only his physical strength but also the warmth of his regard. They had become close during the Sun Hung Kai investigation, and she deeply liked him. Yet, their father-daughter relationship was complicated by the fact that she had been running the inquiry on behalf of the police. And she had been aware of his attraction to her.

In that case, Victoria had immediately realized how much Harvey wanted to know the truth and was willing to cooperate. She was glad to have built a trusting relationship with him, and she hoped it might allow them to work together to the resolve the current case.

"It's been a long time, Mr. Lee."

"Please, call me Harvey. Mr. Lee makes me feel too old. Nice to see you again, Victoria. I hope our work this evening will shed some light on the death of Bertrand Wilmington, which is still a mystery to me. Could we spend a few minutes in my office before going to the trading floor?"

Victoria's reputation for solving complex financial cases had grown since she had dismantled Sun Hung Kai Properties and earned the nickname the Flying Dragon (she was born under the Chinese sign of the dragon). Confronting the management of Sun Hung Kai owners, the powerful Kwok brothers, and a former senior Hong Kong government official, Raphael Lui, for corruption and bribery had not been easy. Nobody had dared to question the integrity of the second largest fortune in Hong Kong. But Victoria had, and several key executives were arrested. The news sent shock waves through the city and had been the focus of intense public attention ever since. At the end of 2014, the brothers were sentenced to five years' in prison, and Raphael Lui got seven and a half years.

Among the things BHS hadn't forgotten in constructing its building were accommodations for its senior executives, which were large but without luxury. Harvey's had a number of contemporary Chinese paintings. *He has taste,* thought Victoria, *and he knows how to create a beautiful environment for his work.* His office had soul and energy.

"We have strictly limited who has been informed of the internal inquiry. We have to act quickly and discreetly." Harvey gestured to the two executives at the table. "Mary Li runs our audit department, and Ravi Subramanian is responsible for the IT that supports the fixed-income and derivatives departments. I believe that the four of us should be able to have a closer look at the transactions that preceded Bertrand Wilmington's death. Mary, why don't you summarize what we already know?"

Victoria interrupted, "Mary, have we worked together at CITIC?"

"Yes. I was in charge of the accounting audit team there ten years ago."

Victoria smiled, "I thought we had met before. I was working at the audit practice for fixed income at CITIC when you were there. What a small world."

"Of course, I remember now. You started as an intern and were so impressive that we immediately hired you," Mary joked.

"Let's catch up one day soon," Victoria replied sincerely.

Mary continued with the case. "Getting down to business, Bertrand approached me two days before his death. He was extremely nervous and looked frightened. He told me he could not have the attention of fixed-income's back office and that his trading book had been activated by some trades from our proprietary account.

He was concerned by the amounts and by the fact that he was on the client side and therefore had nothing to do with the firm's capital positions."

"What was his exact function?"

"He ran the derivatives desk. As you know, derivatives were so exposed during the financial crisis that his activities were constantly scrutinized. He didn't mind transparency, but he also wanted to protect his clients, some of which were politically or financially delicate to handle."

"Did you act upon his initiative?" Victoria asked.

"We decided to look into the matter the same day. We listened to the tapes of the main players. Without Bertrand's knowledge, I asked a couple of my auditors to look at the movements in his account from the previous week and to report to me the next morning."

"The result of their inquiry was indeed worrying." Mary explained. "They found that the irregular trades from account 1130-01 had been executed through Bertrand's accounts." Mary reminded Victoria that this practice was totally prohibited for fear that the proprietary desk might use clients' accounts as appendixes of its own positions. In short, the proprietary desk could not trade ahead of the bank's customers.

Victoria realized the gravity of the irregularities. Had Bertrand been caught executing those trades, he would have immediately been fired, and BHS would have had to report that infraction the same day to the SFC. This was why Bertrand was so scared. His whole career, and more, was at stake.

Mary continued. At Bertrand's request, the head of the proprietary desk, John Highbridge, and the head of the back office, David Chen, were called in for a meeting with Bertrand and Henry Chang.

"Do you mean that Henry Chang was involved in those discussions prior to Bertrand's death?" Victoria asked.

"Yes, and he was instrumental in handling the problem. After all, the fixed-income and derivatives trading positions were at stake."

Victoria wondered why Henry had never mentioned that meeting to her. He must have thought she wouldn't find out or that it might cast doubts about his supervision. The way Henry had presented the facts had given her the impression that it was the first time Bertrand Wilmington had requested the assistance of the compliance department.

Despite her desire to do so, Victoria could not bring this discrepancy up now without disclosing the identity of Pegasus's client, something she would never do unless forced by the authorities. She kept it to herself and planned to confront Henry about it at their meeting the next day. She had absolutely no doubt that Mary Li was honest. Why had Henry not mentioned this?

Victoria felt betrayed. She had repeatedly told Henry that she could only be helpful if he was candid. Here, he was personally involved, with Bertrand Wilmington, in a meeting requested by Bertrand and attended by parties in the audit and compliance departments. She knew how unusual such a request was. Henry's involvement gave the whole inquiry a different turn. The problems had already been shared with the supervisory teams of BHS prior to

Bertrand's death. How could those teams have concluded that it was a suicide without interrogating the participants of the meeting? Were they trying to protect the bank?

"What did you find out?" Victoria asked.

"There seems to have been a triangular set of transactions between the proprietary desk, Bertrand's trading, and one of his most important clients in China, the Chongqing Hedge Fund."

"Is that the fund operated by the municipality, the one that was at the center of the corruption scandal affecting the mayor?"

The mayor had been arrested for corruption, his wife had been accused of killing an employee, and they were separately tried and jailed in a public tribunal. The Chinese leadership had used them as an example to demonstrate their commitment to sanctions against corruption at the highest level. The Chongqing Hedge Fund was apparently at the center of the movements of cash to and from the municipality.

"Yes."

"Did the Chinese authorities know about that account?" Victoria asked.

"Not only do they know of its existence," Harvey said, "but we regularly communicate requested information about that account. Our business between China and Hong Kong is so important that, as our clients from Mainland China know, we cannot refuse Mainland authorities' official requests for information if they pertain their entities. This policy was cleared at the highest echelons of the bank and has the approval of the Bank of England and Her Majesty's Treasury. The Chancellor of the Exchequer receives the same information as the Chinese government. We are a UK bank, after all."

"A bit like the Swiss bank and US taxation authorities?"

"Yes," Harvey said. "Bertrand was not aware of the connection until a few days before his death. We could not disclose such sensitive political information. We had to protect the bank and the individual."

Harvey had taken a risk by disclosing such sensitive information to Victoria. It could easily backfire as a breach of secrecy in a public inquiry. He needed to do it, however, to give her the full picture of what happed on the twenty-second floor.

"To be sure I understand the situation," Victoria clarified, "was Bertrand dealing with the Chongqing Hedge Fund in derivatives and discovered something that bothered him? A direct transfer from the proprietary account to the client?"

"Exactly. However, we do not know precisely what he discovered. He was transparent with us, but he might not have had time to inform us of the details of his findings. He had no access to confidential data that were uncovered by the audit department."

"Who was ultimately responsible for the Chongqing Hedge Fund's account in fixed income?"

"Henry Chang is the account manager for the various Mainland government agencies for all matters pertaining to fixed-income and derivatives operations."

Victoria could see the whole picture more clearly now. It was time to get down to the details of Bertrand Wilmington's activities. They all left Harvey's office and went to the trading room. Victoria was increasingly puzzled by the importance of the elements of the story that Henry had not disclosed to her. It confirmed her suspicions that he was trying to manipulate Pegasus to cover himself. What was he trying to hide? More than ever, he looked like a prime suspect in Bertrand's death.

23

T<small>HERE WAS SOMETHING MAGICAL ABOUT AN EMPTY TRADING</small> room, Victoria thought, and seeing one at sunset made it even more striking. She felt that, at any time, music might start playing and cartoon characters would fill the space. It was hard to imagine what the room looked like when two to three thousand employees occupied the space, trading billions of Hong Kong dollars per hour.

The derivatives traders were positioned next to the fixed-income traders. Their sales forces and back offices were on the opposite side of the room. While the two departments complemented each other, they each maintained their own profit and loss accounts to prevent giving one department a competitive advantage over the other. It was not a regulatory rule, only a business rule implemented in the interest of BHS and its clients.

As Victoria sat at Bertrand Wilmington's desk, she could almost feel his distress from the days before his death. The note was still there: "Better leave . . ." What had he discovered that he or others couldn't bear? She knew the pressure that traders faced these days. Since the financial crisis, the scrutiny they were subjected to had become so tedious that people in their positions felt they were constantly under suspicion.

The IT manager, Ravi Subramanian, had unlocked the screens, and the list of transactions scrolled before Victoria's eyes. She sorted them by account. The amounts of several accounts with similar first numbers clearly outpaced others.

"These are the Chinese government agencies," Ravi said.

"They all start with 888. The Chongqing Hedge Fund ends with 99," Mary Li said.

"So Bertrand traded with several important Mainland accounts?"

"Yes. There are very few firms that can trade in the right volume for such agencies. As head of the derivatives department, he handled fifty very large accounts."

Victoria noticed that some amounts had been transferred from the proprietary trading account directly to the Chongqing Hedge Fund. These were the trades that Bertrand Wilmington had discovered and brought to the attention of his supervisors.

"How is it possible that the 1130-01 account could trade directly with clients without transiting through the trader's book?" Victoria asked. "Bertrand should have made decisions about those."

"We still don't know how it happened and who did it," Harvey Lee said. "That is the subject of our inquiry. Only John Highbridge or David Chen could authorize such trades. We are also looking at the reasons why the back office didn't block this trade."

Having worked at CITIC, an institution owned by the State Council of the People's Republic of China, Victoria knew that these transactions would be known to the Chinese authorities, who would monitor such cases closely.

"Bertrand didn't know he was handling the account of the Chongqing Hedge Fund. Henry was the account manager, so only he knew the identity of the account holders."

"But Bertrand knew his clients belonged to the Chinese public-sector, right?" Victoria asked.

"Yes. That's all he knew," Harvey concluded.

"Ravi, could you print out the trades Bertrand made with the Chongqing Hedge Fund?"

While the documents printed, Victoria walked around the room. She was so familiar with those desks, each cohabited by three wide screens and pictures of partners, spouses and children. It was fascinating to see the decorative differences between women's and men's desks. She smiled at a kangaroo toy similar to the one she still kept on her desk. Behind each of these desks were human stories of families, friends, and home. Despite the pressure of their work, members of the trading community maintained solidarity and friendship that could play a critical role in their lives, for better or worse.

"Here are the print-outs," Ravi said.

Victoria sat with her feet on a desk and the paper on her legs, focused and concentrated in the same position she sat in when she had worked in a bank. Suddenly her attention was drawn to the Chongqing Hedge Fund account number.

"How is this possible?"

"What do you mean?" Mary Li asked.

Victoria turned to Ravi.

"How do you display the account numbers on the traders' screens? Do you include hyphens, periods, and commas?"

"On paper, yes. Not on traders' screens," explained Ravi. "There, the full account number is only used for execution, to reach the client account."

"Look at the account numbers," said Victoria. "The hyphen falls in sixth position of this number while the Chinese agencies have it immediately after the initial 888. This seems to mean that BHS never actually traded with the Chongqing Hedge Fund directly."

When she was at CITIC, Victoria discovered a similar scheme between CITIC and the Chinese government. Needless to say, CITIC was hugely embarrassed. It wasn't supposed to come to light in Hong Kong. The company was happy to see her leave but probably less happy when she joined the police force. It was the only place where CITIC couldn't hunt her. That's how she survived. It made her certain that there was some irregularity in the way the account was opened.

Victoria explained. "From an IT standpoint, the difference in hyphen placement is irrelevant. However, from an account management standpoint, it means that what we all thought was an account of the Chongqing Hedge Fund might belong to somebody else."

"That makes no sense," Mary said. "We know that the transactions are for the hedge fund. We have a direct relationship with the fund managers."

"Could the account you knew as the Chongqing account be, in fact, the personal account of another entity? That would allow fraud in a number of ways." Victoria thought for a moment. "Does BHS receive the account statements from the fund or from this entity?"

"We don't know what the real portfolio is," Ravi answered. "We use the Hong Kong Stock Exchange clearing system. Are you telling us that the account called the Chongqing Hedge Fund could have been an intermediary account before reaching the proper account?"

"Possibly. You should be able to find out through the phantom account's statements. Between your account and the actual Chongqing Hedge Fund's account, a lot can happen."

"And the system does not display the dissimilarity," Ravi acknowledged.

"Exactly," said Victoria.

A long silence followed. This could have incalculable consequences not only for the firm but also for the individuals involved. Victoria scrutinized the accounts.

"We need to have access to the original account documents," Harvey said. "The original documents related to the Chinese government accounts are kept in a safe in London by request of the Chinese government, which did not want those documents to be accessible in Hong Kong. I'll call our group general counsel first. It will take a couple of hours for them to locate the actual documents, but the seven-hour time difference gives us the chance to find out what could have happened before the end of their business day."

As Victoria sat in Harvey Lee's office, it was beginning to sink in that the case involved way more than a normal trading problem. BHS might lose the accounts of the Chinese agencies if the Chinese Central Bank—the People's Bank of China, or PBOC—found any ir-regularities. Nobody could afford to cross the governor of the PBOC. Chairman Zhou Xiaochuan was an honest and well-mannered human being, but he would not compromise on something as fundamental as phantom accounts.

"Do you mean that, if there is a phantom account, the fund man-agers of the Municipality of Chongqing could have used it to divert some of those monies to other beneficiaries?" Harvey asked.

"Possibly. The China Securities Regulation Commission should be able to reconcile the amounts with our numbers and figure out, if not where it went, at least how much was siphoned."

"Who in Chongqing would know about this?"

"Definitely the mayor and, of course, his cronies and beneficiaries. But there might be others who could possibly blackmail the leadership of the municipality," Victoria noted.

"We will need to fully cooperate with them, even if the matter must be handled in Hong Kong. I don't know what to say, Victoria. We have been working on this for almost two weeks now, and we did not focus on the account number."

"Nobody does, Harvey. It is so tricky and well hidden."

"I understand why Francis insisted that I give you access."

"Without it, I wouldn't have been able to focus on these accounts."

"We should have. Sometimes IT sophistication makes us forget that we always need to go back to the original piece of paper. Let me walk you out. I need to do my homework now."

They silently went through the exit. Victoria thought of Bertrand Wilmington. Had he discovered something he was not supposed to know? Was this why Henry Chang went to Shanghai? Could Bertrand have threatened him? Was the mystery transaction affecting Bertrand's colleagues or the Chinese authorities? Was it fraud, forgery, or both?

A car was waiting for Victoria by the curb.

"It's my car," Harvey said. "I won't need it for a while."

He put his arm around her shoulder. Under normal circumstances, she would have rebuffed the gesture, but tonight, after the ordeal at the Macau restaurant, she was grateful for the tenderness. She laid her head on his shoulder and hugged him.

"Thank you, Harvey. You are a gentleman. I'll take the car home. I need some rest." She gave him an encouraging smile. "Please call me when you have the information from London."

Harvey wished he were twenty years younger. Victoria was so attractive . . . he waved to the detective as she drove away. She provided critical information to his inquiry. But if she was correct, Bertrand Wilmington's death had unpredictable consequences that tied back to the Mainland.

Victoria reflected on how much class many older men like Harvey possessed. It was so comforting. She had once been seduced by such a man and always remembered the experience with fondness. Of course, he was married with a few children. At least he never pretended he would divorce his wife and marry Victoria.

Harvey Lee's car, a late-model Jaguar XJ, was comfortable and unusual in her part of Kowloon. She attracted some attention on her way home but enjoyed the ride.

24

VICTORIA WAS AMAZED AS SHE SORTED THROUGH WHAT WAS RE-
ally behind the Chongqing Hedge Fund account. She looked through
the information she had about it. Its Chinese name was Chongqing
Yuxin, and it had been created by the municipality to invest in the
city's listed companies. Most of the capital had been subscribed by
various municipal agencies, but thirty-five percent was reported to
be held privately.

Victoria fell asleep quickly but was awoken at five in the morning
when Harvey Lee called.

"Did I wake you up?" he asked.

"Yes, but it is fine. Have you found something?"

"Indeed. You were right. Our account for the Chongqing Hedge
Fund was a phantom account. It looks so much like the original that
we missed the tiny difference in the hyphenation of its account number. Since those don't appear on the screen, all Chinese government
agencies look alike to traders. The original hard copy in London isn't
perfectly clear, but it seems to indicate that the account number might
have been altered. The London office is doing a laboratory analysis.
We will know the results tomorrow."

"Who signed the account-opening papers?" Victoria asked.

"David Chen and Henry Chang."

"How interesting. Their fingerprints are all over this affair. What are you going to do?"

"I need to go to Shanghai immediately," Harvey replied. "I have to explain to the authorities what happened in person. Doing so is never pleasant, but we have serious credibility with them for one reason: we always tell them what we know. It makes no sense to play cat and mouse with regulators. You always lose. They have all the leverage. They know we try our best to identify fraud on both sides of the Pearl River. However, if Bertrand Wilmington had discovered the discrepancy, those who benefited from it would have had an interest in eliminating him."

"He might have exposed himself?" Victoria inquired.

"Bertrand had spoken with David Chen as well as with Henry Chang. They were the only two who knew about it. We will tighten our internal inquiry, but people connected to the Chongqing Hedge Fund must have taken a significant slice of the profits. Hopefully, nobody at BHS was part of the conspiracy."

"Why are you going to Shanghai rather than Chongqing?"

"The oversight of hedge funds is in the hands of CSRC's Shanghai office. I might need to go to Beijing later in the month, too. We need to find out who is behind the scheme. It is essential for everybody."

"Keep me posted. This is taking a totally different turn than I expected, but it might explain Bertrand's death. He wouldn't be the first broker dealing with Chinese public agencies to be eliminated under strange conditions."

After she hung up, it didn't make sense for Victoria to go back to sleep. She decided to take another long bath while listening to her favorite jazz singer, Diana Krall. As she got in the tub, some of her wounds stung. It would be a few weeks before she completely recovered. The warm water and her bubble bath soothed her. She left the faucet running to maintain the temperature and thought about the investigation.

The fact that it had taken such a drastic turn didn't particularly surprise her. She had enough experience to know that the unexpected always happened.

However, the new information added a heavy and delicate burden. What had started as a pure criminal investigation was now very sensitive, especially because it concerned corruption, a hot topic for Mainland China and a political tool for the president in his complex web of relationships.

Victoria now had to consider that Bertrand's death might have been initiated in Chongqing or Beijing. Which executives at BHS were connected enough that China could use them to eliminate Bertrand?

It was now up to BHS to act, and Harvey Lee was right to act quickly and remain directly in touch with the police commissioner and the SFC. Would he be able to convince them to reopen the inquiry into Bertrand Wilmington's death? That would definitely depend on the depth of his personal conviction. At this stage, he needed to remain neutral until more evidence emerged.

Victoria looked forward to seeing Henry Chang that day. He had intimate knowledge of the accounts and their managers, and she was ready to find out what he really knew and had so far hid from her.

25

Victoria waited in her office for the important visitor. She was prepared not only to listen to him but also to challenge him for misleading her. She didn't take obfuscation lightly. She was tense, like a warrior ready to fight.

Henry Chang arrived on time, dapper as always in his double-breasted suit. He looked as if he were arriving for a date. Victoria examined his reflection in a mirror as he waited in the comfortable lobby armchairs. He was so sure of himself. She asked Judy Wang to bring him to Sir Francis's conference room.

"How have things been since we met last week?" Victoria asked as she entered.

"Pretty good. I went to Bali for two days. Helena is shooting a movie there, and I wanted to be around for some scenes I was uncomfortable with."

"Violent?"

"No, erotic."

"Really? That shouldn't be new to her. She's not known for being shy on camera. I saw her last movie at a hotel; it tread the fine line between erotic and romantic. She is really glamorous."

"I just don't want her to get carried away by her French co-star!

We're not married yet, and an actor is a potential challenger. She seems to like him too much for my taste."

"You know how to handle it, and I'm sure you're not inactive in Hong Kong when she's away. You have so many lady friends. How could you be jealous?"

Henry was the archetype of the Don Juan. He could not resist Victoria's cheap flattery. He was like a panting dog. He felt so irresistible that he did not see the arrow coming his way. Judy brought in green tea as Henry and Victoria stared at each other from across the table. It reminded Victoria of a police interrogation. She smiled inside. It was time for her to turn the tables.

"How much do you know about Bertrand Wilmington's trading activities?"

"Very little," Henry answered. "We all have our own accounts and don't pay much attention to others."

"Why are you lying to me?"

Victoria stared daggers at Henry. The look seemed to frighten him. She was the Flying Dragon. This was a former police officer interrogating a suspect. Henry had no place to hide.

Victoria continued. "Why didn't you tell me that Bertrand Wilmington's accounts were mostly Chinese government accounts? Why didn't you tell me that you went to Shanghai for one of Bertrand's accounts? Why didn't you tell me that you attended a meeting with audit and compliance?"

"Was it important?"

"Of course it was. Are you stupid or a liar? You know I can't accomplish my mandate if you're not transparent with me. Don't play with me, Henry. You're in muddy waters now, and if you want some help, you have to tell me what you know."

Victoria had clearly managed to destabilize Henry. She knew so much about Bertrand's connections with China, and in only three days. This was one of the best-kept secrets at BHS.

"Who told you that?"

"Sir Francis asked Harvey Lee to let me go to BHS last night. I spent a very interesting evening with members of the audit, compliance, and IT departments in the trading room. You remember, we were supposed to go there on Monday."

"I'm sorry. I completely forgot."

"Forgot or chose not to deliver, Henry? I'll say it again: don't play games with me. Is that why you went to Shanghai in a hurry?"

"It wasn't in a hurry. It had been planned for weeks."

Victoria was fuming. Despite what she said, he was still trying to mislead her. That combination of stupidity, arrogance, and disrespect for her was unbearable. Who was he trying to fool here?

"You are lying, Mr. Chang. You were supposed to be on vacation that day, according to your calendar. Did you go to Shanghai for your own business?"

"How do you know all this? Who talked to you? This is insane!"

"What game are you playing? Why did you hire Pegasus?"

"I did not hire Pegasus. I hired you! Diana convinced me that if somebody could find out what happened, it would be you. I'm trying to save my skin. You don't know what is behind all this. I could be killed or arrested at any moment. I thought you would trust me."

"Bullshit! You're still lying to me! What do you know about the Chongqing mayor and his cronies?"

26

HENRY WAS TRAPPED. HE HAD LIED TO VICTORIA, AND SHE NOW second-guessed anything he told her. He could no longer manipulate her to pursue his objectives. Diana had told him that he wouldn't be able to fool Victoria, but he had thought he knew better. There was only one way out: telling Victoria the truth.

"I went to Shanghai at the request of the fund managers. They were concerned that the dual structure of the account might have been discovered. They thought someone in Hong Kong might have discovered the plot." Henry then recounted the entire story.

His meeting in Shanghai had not gone well at all, and the Chinese officials he met had been brutal. But he was on BHS's mission. The meeting also included intermediaries from the mayor's office who received some of the commissions from the lucrative Chongqing Hedge Fund account. Some of the recent trades had raised eyebrows, and the intermediaries were furious that Bertrand Wilmington had exposed the scheme.

Rather than over a lavish luncheon at the Grand Hyatt in Pudong, the meeting took place in the intermediaries' offices across the river so that it could be completely private.

The intermediaries' leader was Wang Chi, a graduate of New York

University's Stern Business School who had spent five years at the infamous SAC Capital, Steven Cohen's hedge fund that had just been investigated. He had the classical style of hedge fund traders. A US citizen of Chinese descent, Wang Chi had been hired by the mayor of Chongqing himself. He always wore dark glasses and was impossible to read. He could be as pleasant as he could be ruthless. He looked just as much like a mobster as he did a banker. In fact, all those present resembled members of La Cosa Nostra.

"How did Bertrand find out about the identity of the account?" Wang Chi growled.

"I don't know," Henry said. "I certainly didn't tell him anything."

"I don't believe you."

"It's the truth. Bertrand was being harassed by some guys at the office and was extremely nervous. He noticed that direct proprietary trades were going straight to the Chongqing account. His book was obviously being hacked or manipulated."

"Did he talk to you about it?" Wang Chi asked.

"Yes, of course. This kind of trade is strictly prohibited under Hong Kong regulations. So he tried to find out the origin."

"He knows too much!"

"I agree," Henry replied. "Bertrand told me he suspected that the BHS account, might be a phantom account. I don't believe he suspects anybody in particular. He was much more worried about regulation and bullying than he was by the Chongqing trading account. I assume that the investigation will cast some light on the subject."

"Investigation? What investigation?! Does anybody else at BHS know anything?"

"A few days ago, Bertrand went to see Mary Li, who heads our audit department, to report the proprietary transactions. She is smart and fearless. This is standard procedure. They launched an audit, which is also standard procedure. Harvey Lee, the general counsel, also launched an internal investigation into the fixed-income department's practices."

"Do you know anything else about Bertrand?" Wang Chi inquired.

"Other than that he's gay, I don't have any information about his private life. You're wrong about him. He is not dangerous. He is candid with me, and he's naive."

Wang Chi jumped from his chair and erupted. "Naive and candid people are the most dangerous! They are totally uncontrollable. If this gets out, we'll be arrested for corruption and probably executed. Our lives are on the line! Do you understand what this means, you idiot?! Do you know that nobody is allowed to stop Harvey Lee's investigation? He is close to the CSRC and considered to be the most incorruptible person in the banking industry."

Wang Chi and his associates looked at each other with disbelief. Without another word, they immediately left for the airport.

Henry stopped and watched Victoria as she tapped notes on her iPad at the speed of light.

"What was the conclusion of the meeting?" Victoria asked when she had finished.

"The fund managers told me, 'Harvey is bad news. However, we must first deal with Bertrand. He must be eliminated one way or another. He knows too much and is now protected by the investigation. He is a threat to all of us.' I left the meeting convinced that they meant murder. Those guys know how to eliminate troublemakers."

A long silence followed.

Then Victoria went on the attack. "Why did you not tell me you took part in the audit meeting?"

"I didn't believe it was important."

"Stop lying to me, Henry! This was the last and most important audit and compliance meeting before Bertrand Wilmington's death. You were his boss, yet you 'forgot' to tell me? What else are you hiding?"

"I really feel threatened. I was hoping you could defuse this time bomb and protect me against further investigation. Instead, you seem to be on their side! I need your help!"

"It's too late. Now you have to play it straight, Henry. Nobody can control what is going on any longer. If there is a criminal investigation for murder, you are an obvious suspect, and anything can be held against you. How will you convince anybody that you didn't push Bertrand out of that window under the orders of one of your largest clients from the Mainland?"

"I did not kill Bertrand!"

"I wish I could believe you, Henry. But you are such a manipulator that I cannot distinguish the truth from what you would like me to believe. As far as I am concerned, your innocence will need to be proved. And you might have a hard time convincing the police force, let alone a jury or the court."

At that moment, Laura Woo and Sir Francis entered the conference room and introduced themselves. Then they dropped the bomb: they had been listening over the internal audio system.

Henry stood furiously and headed toward the door.

"You only have one exit, Henry," Sir Francis said with authority. "You need to meet as soon as possible with Harvey Lee and confess everything. He is your only hope for survival. I talked to him. He will see you when he comes back from Shanghai. He left early this morning."

These quiet words left no doubt about the strength of his advice.

"You may have managed to finesse the IPO market when I was at the SFC," Laura Woo added, "but this situation is very different. One of your colleagues was probably murdered."

Henry thought for a moment before he spoke. "You are probably right," he relented. "In the meantime, I'll go back to the office."

"I don't think so," Victoria said.

"What do you mean?"

"Until you meet with Harvey Lee, all your credentials have been deactivated. Your computer is being searched, and your VPN access has been severed."

Henry knew he was in a terrible mess. Not being able to access the BHS's VPN was the kiss of death. His umbilical cord had been cut. God only knew what they would uncover.

"Why don't you tell us more about what you know of the scam?" Victoria said. "Who are the parties to the intermediary structure who were getting cash? It might help us give you advice."

What Henry explained next was even more surprising than Victoria, Sir Francis or Laura Woo could have imagined. Pure corruption. Ten percent of every payment made to the phantom intermediary would never reach the Chongqing Hedge Fund. It was automatically distributed to the "sponsors" of the fund. Over the past three months, more than one hundred million dollars had been diverted—a significantly greater amount than China required to execute those found guilty.

Bertrand Wilmington had discovered the traffic the week before his death, but Henry had convinced him that there was no need to contact the compliance department. When David Chen had started corrupting his trades, Bertrand went on his own to the audit department. Henry had been squeezed on both sides from the Chongqing gang and BHS.

⸻

After the interrogation, Victoria and Henry headed to her office. He admired her strength as much as he hated it. He could recognize a pro from a hundred yards away.

"Why did you approach me?" Victoria asked.

"I was hoping you would limit your involvement to the gay conspiracy theory and a few irregular trades that didn't affect me. It was my only hope to divert attention from my involvement in the Bertrand Wilmington drama."

Victoria wondered again why Henry Chang had broken up with Diana Yu. Could it have had anything to do with professional circumstances? Had he ever shared these with Diana? Was this why Diana had come to her?

"Is this why you broke up with Diana?"

"Yes. The Chongqing managers discovered that I was in a relationship with her and that she was at the Hong Kong Police Force fraud department. They told me I had to break up with her if I wanted to continue to work with them."

"You are an abuser, Henry. Why didn't you tell her? Do you have no decency? You are wealthy enough without these conspiracies. Now you're in danger of being accused of corruption, conspiracy and murder! What kind of human being are you?"

It felt good to let her anger out. Victoria didn't need the answers; her intuition was like a laser beam. Her eyes scrutinized Henry. He looked pathetic and defenseless.

It was time for him to leave. What he had most feared was crashing down around him. Even dead, Bertrand had managed to reveal the fraud.

If Diana Yu were to be involved in the fraud investigation, Henry would lose. He hated to be squeezed by two women. If there was one thing he couldn't tolerate, it was being ruled by a woman, and now he was ruled by two. Henry hated women's ability to control him ever since he was a child in a house dominated by women. Despite all that, he knew perfectly well that Diana and Victoria were probably the only two people who could tell his story in a credible way. It was time to face the consequences of his actions.

Victoria could almost read his mind. Ever since adolescence, she had been confronted with aggression when men felt controlled or manipulated. Their self-esteem was sometimes so low that they even resorted to using physical strength to prove their dominance. Weren't they all *zhiloahu* (paper tigers)?

27

Harvey Lee took a shower at the office, where he kept a travel kit. He had only slept for a couple of hours on his office sofa. Harvey deeply hated this kind of emergency action but knew too well that time was of the essence.

Harvey headed straight to Hong Kong International Airport to catch the first Dragonair flight to Shanghai. He had contacted the head of the CSRC in Shanghai, James Liu, who had set the meeting for the morning at City Hall. Deputy Mayor Shi Lai, who had been running the Shanghai Stock Exchange and the CSRC's Shanghai office, was hosting the meeting.

The high-level meeting would be intensely political. John Wilcox had agreed that it was probably better that Harvey go alone. John had to keep his powder dry for a possible Beijing confrontation.

Harvey was more than aware of the dangers of this inquiry and the stakes of the meeting. He needed to make sure that BHS would not be blamed by the Mainland regulators. He got a message from Victoria: "When are you coming back from Shanghai?"

Harvey couldn't help but smile at her omnipresence in an investigation. Victoria also had a lot at stake. This was turning violent and confusing and could hurt her physically. There was nothing he could do to protect her, but he certainly felt that he owed her solid support. Victoria had identified the minute element that had been critical to the progress of the inquiry. Harvey was concerned that the Chongqing forces might have been responsible for Bertrand Wilmington's death. For them, this was a matter of life and death. Could they still be trying to derail the investigation? Was the Macau restaurant attack part of that?

When Harvey landed in Shanghai and deplaned, security officers took him in an official car straight to Shanghai City Hall, where he arrived five minutes early. He was rushed to a room, and soon after Deputy Mayor Shi joined him with the CSRC team.

It was very unusual for these men to meet together without their armies of advisors and assistants. Confidentiality was definitely necessary today.

"Hello, Harvey," Shi said. "We were expecting you sooner."

"But I arrived five minutes early."

"That's not what I mean," Shi said with a big smile. "I thought we would have had the pleasure of meeting you soon after the death of your colleague Bertrand Wilmington."

"I understand what you mean, Deputy Mayor Shi," Harvey replied. "But why would I need to come and see you about his death?"

"I know that the Hong Kong police concluded that it was a suicide, but they had no idea of the sensitive activities of your colleague and could not connect the dots, for good reasons. This makes it as much a Mainland matter as a Hong Kong matter."

"I thought that the Chongqing account was monitored by the CSRC, not by the municipality." Harvey smiled. "I am here today because we only just found the evidence you are suggesting last night."

Harvey Lee explained meticulously the mechanism through which ten percent of the funds were siphoned by the Chongqing management team. He knew that the CSRC was as guilty of negligence as BHS. They needed to resolve the case with as little noise and politics as possible.

"So the discrepancy stems from the fact that, electronically, the two accounts look exactly the same, seen from Hong Kong," James Liu said. "It will look different seen from Chongqing and probably even from Shanghai. You are expecting the laboratory results this afternoon, I suppose?"

"Is Henry your agent?" Harvey asked, still putting the pieces together in his head.

"Not really," Liu answered, "but when we suspected that the Chongqing Hedge Fund was the conduit of the fraud, we started following Henry more closely. He came to Shanghai the day before Bertrand Wilmington's death to meet the three fund managers. We were concerned about that meeting, but it was cleared in Beijing."

"What was your concern?" Harvey asked.

"Mostly that they could have killed Henry Chang, who is, as you know, the key Hong Kong executive in your bank dealing with the official agencies."

"I didn't realize the importance of that meeting for you," Harvey confessed.

"Henry informed them about your inquiry, and they turned violent," Liu said. "They knew that nothing would stop you and that we probably knew about it too. That's why the meeting ended abruptly."

Pressed by the political heat, Harvey Lee asked, "Did you have all the evidence you needed?"

"Enough to arrest the three managers at the airport when they tried to board a plane to Chongqing. One of them called their boss on his mobile when they left the meeting with Henry. We taped that conversation and the meeting."

"I wish we could do that sometimes," Harvey said.

"You know, your democratic system is not necessarily as efficient as ours," Shi said. "What we need now is to reconcile the official and the phantom accounts to figure out how much was siphoned off and who got the money. We need to work with you for that. But we will take care of the reconciliation of the positions."

"We will compare notes. I assume this is an official CSRC inquiry. As you know, we do not have the real accounts of the funds. We only know the intermediate account. Would you like to come over, or can your inquiry be done electronically?"

"Yes, it is an official request," Liu interjected. "We will inform the SFC. We are limiting our role to that part of the case for now. We will let the SFC and the Hong Kong Police Force take care of the necessary actions for two weeks. If they don't uncover the necessary information, we will need to interfere, but I count on you to ensure that things get solved before that is necessary."

"Commissioner Chu and I spoke about it," Shi added. "I believe you, Harvey, have an important meeting with the commissioner. As for reconciling the accounts, doing so electronically could create problems of confidentiality. Here is the disk. Everything is on there."

Harvey was always stunned by the speed at which information passed between Hong Kong and Shanghai. Despite the two systems, financial fraud had become a new area of close cooperation since the arrival of President Xi Liping, who had made anticorruption one of his main priorities. It had also become a key priority for regulators since the Chongqing mayor's arrest.

"Can we close the intermediate account and deal directly with the Chongqing fund?" Harvey asked.

"Soon, yes, but not yet," Liu responded. "There are a couple of irregular transactions that need to hit the account first so we can identify some of the beneficiaries. Then, our investigation will be closed."

"How long will it take?"

"It is a question of a few days. In the meantime, we want BHS to continue what it is doing for the fund. The arrests have not yet been made public. Those accounts going to another bank would make things worse."

"What does that mean for BHS?" Harvey asked.

"The CSRC is making no allegations against BHS. It is amazing that the mechanism of the fraud could be so simple. Hong Kong will have to deal with it."

"I was stunned myself when it was discovered," Harvey admitted. "We have the most sophisticated systems to avoid such frauds, but the devil is definitely in the details."

"How did you find out?"

"A detective from Pegasus, Victoria Leung, was working for one of their clients on a related investigation. Her background in the audit department of CITIC and at the fraud department of the Hong Kong Police Force helped her identify the characteristics of the Mainland public accounts."

"Are you talking about the Flying Dragon?" Liu asked.

"Yes. How do you know her?" Harvey Lee was surprised that the Chinese authorities knew of her.

"We followed the Sun Hung Kai inquiry closely, and the way she managed to confound the Kwok brothers was a real coup. We also use Pegasus ourselves on some issues with the United Kingdom. The MI5 agents are so well trained. We even send them trainees. Laura Woo is advising them and previously built our internal governance system. Very interesting woman."

Harvey grinned. "You really are everywhere, James."

"I have a final question for you," Liu said. "Do you believe that Bertrand Wilmington's death could have been provoked by people connected to Chongqing?"

"I have no information on that. However, I certainly would not rule that out. We are dealing with gangsters armed and financed by the municipality. The related timing of Henry Chang's visit to Shanghai and Bertrand Wilmington's death troubles me. It is too much of a coincidence."

"Nobody can pretend to be unaffected by those crimes. Corruption has become a global problem. We are all in the same boat. We need to combine forces to stop them. We will never be able to eradicate the problem alone."

The meeting was surreal.

Here the three of them were, in the fortress of the municipality of Shanghai—the most powerful in China and maybe in the world—talking as if these matters were business as usual. At stake was the resolution of one of the most sensitive scandals in the history of China.

"Thank you," Harvey said. "This is helpful. We should be able to come to closure within the next two weeks."

Shi Lai and James Liu accompanied their guest to the car, and Harvey Lee was back to his office by five in the evening for a meeting with Henry Chang. While waiting for Henry, he instructed his assistant to organize a meeting with all players on Thursday afternoon. He needed twenty-four hours.

Harvey next called Victoria Leung. He needed information that he could not get from his own people without risking spreading sensitive information through the organization.

"Good evening, Victoria. Are you recovering?"

"I'm fine. Thank you for asking. How was your meeting?"

"Complicated. I'll fill you in on the details. But first, I need your help. I can no longer dismiss the idea that Bertrand Wilmington's death might have been instigated by Chongqing. This is not my field, but I know that Pegasus has connections that may know more, and I do not want the police involved. The coincidence is too strange."

"I understand. I've also been worried about it. After all, we're all relying on Henry Chang's account of the meeting."

"Shanghai taped everything and they cannot exclude it either."

"Let me see what I can do," Victoria promised.

"I'm about to meet Henry Chang now. I don't intend to mention anything to him. I assume he is your client, but I do not need you to confirm it."

"Thank you. I wouldn't anyway."

Victoria promised Harvey that she would get back to him the next morning. He also told her that the Flying Dragon's reputation had crossed the Pearl River as a result of her involvement in the Kwok scandal.

"I don't know whether to take that as a compliment," Victoria said. "I will certainly keep it in mind. I know that our colleagues in London are involved with Shanghai, although I don't know the details."

"One thing is certain: the repression of financial fraud has become a global business," Harvey lamented.

"So are the banks," Victoria said with a smile that was perceptible over the phone.

Harvey hung up the phone and noticed the laboratory report on the account documents sitting on his desk. He paused for a moment, and then read them. As he had anticipated, the document had been altered prior to being sent to London. David Chen and Henry Chang were the signatories.

28

THAT AFTERNOON, CHRISTINE FREED PARKED HER CAR IN FRONT of one of those beautiful (and extraordinarily expensive) apartment buildings on Hong Kong Peak, overlooking the bay. It was one of the most prodigious views in the world. The district was a world away from the busy downtown: flowers and trees gave it the atmosphere of a wealthy suburb, and swimming pools were plentiful.

Christopher and Catherine Wilmington were expecting Christine. She had indicated that Pegasus was inquiring about the cause of their son's death. They had said that they didn't believe they could help, but the Australian woman was very persuasive and compassionate.

Christopher Wilmington brought Christine up to the penthouse. He suggested that Christine be soft since his wife was still in shock, the way men often pleaded for themselves by using their partners as an excuse. He was a deeply shattered father. Two weeks after Bertrand's death, the wounds were still wide open. Maybe talking about their own questions would soothe their suffering.

Catherine Wilmington stared at the young Australian woman in an attempt to assess what she could expect from Christine. She thought this woman might hurt her. Instead, Christine's eyes and smile reassured Catherine, and she smiled in return. They sat on the terrace and drank tea.

"I am so grateful to you both for receiving me," Christine said. "I feel deeply moved to be with you, and the last thing I want to do is to bring you any further hurt after your irreparable loss."

"Thank you," Christopher said. "It has been an ordeal, but I understand that you're trying to shed some light on the case."

"Yes. There are some aspects surrounding Bertrand's death that we would like to better understand," Christine explained.

"Is there anything we can do? We have been turning over all the possible explanations and haven't find one. Maybe we will have to accept the unacceptable, that . . ." His voice trailed off.

Christine waited for Christopher to collect himself.

"Absolutely," Catherine said. "A week before his death, Bertrand was sitting here and talking about his plans to take a new job away from finance in Sydney. He had found a university program on gender and equality. It was like a dream come true for him. I'm sure you can understand what such a move to your country could mean. Would a young man with such plans voluntarily take his life?"

"That is news to us," Christine said. "How long had he been thinking about going to Australia?"

"At least six months," Christopher answered. "He had become increasingly frustrated by the way he was treated in the trading room, and he had had enough of it. He didn't believe things would change, so he decided to leave that jungle, as he called it. Working there was not worth the money anymore."

"Whom did he contact in Australia?"

"The University of Sydney. He first reached out to them last summer."

"That indeed challenges the suicide motive. I heard that Bertrand had gotten a ticket to Sydney, but we all assumed it was for a holiday. Do you mind if I discuss something more personal that could be a bit uncomfortable?"

"Please, go ahead," Christopher replied.

"Bertrand was very close to a former fellow student at the University of Hong Kong."

"Do you mean Louis Cheung?"

"Yes, Louis Cheung."

"He is such a wonderful kid. Allow me to use that term. The couple that he and Bertrand formed was an example for all couples. Their attachment and honesty was incredibly . . . touching . . ." Catherine broke down into sobs, and her husband took her hand.

These parents are a real couple, Christine thought. Their family had been through the most abominable amputation in losing a child. Their suffering was palpable, and so was their solidarity in pain.

After a long silence, Christopher continued. "It was very difficult for me to accept that my son was gay. Fathers tend to try or hope to make their sons conform to a certain model of masculinity, and rightly or wrongly, I resented his homosexuality as a failure of my own. That is, until my wife and I talked a lot about it. Catherine was much more prepared than I to accept that it was who Bertrand was. It has now been at least five years since we understood what Louis meant to Bertrand and we had truly accepted who he was. Our faith helped us with this. We don't understand how some religions can be against homosexuality. They should be welcoming."

Christine nodded in understanding. "Was Bertrand still with Louis?"

"You probably know that Louis traveled a lot. The travel had interfered with their intimacy, but it certainly did not break their fundamental relationship. They were still very much in love."

"Have you heard from Louis recently?"

"Oh yes. The next morning, he came up here and spent the day with us," Catherine explained. "He is a son-in-law to us. We listened to Bertrand's music, read his poems, and talked about him until late in the night. Louis's presence was wonderful, even though he was completely devastated."

"That must have been very poignant."

"It made a huge difference to the three of us. We hope to stay in touch with him, even if he goes to Australia, as he and Bertrand had originally planned."

Christine was deeply moved by what she had heard and asked to listen to some of Bertrand's music. Catherine connected his iPhone to their system, and Simon and Garfunkel's "The Sound of Silence" filled the room. Christine thought it was very fitting. She stayed for dinner.

In their dignity, Christopher and Catherine were even more inspiring than they would have been had they been crying. They remained connected with their lost child through his legacy. Bertrand was present at the table in a mysterious way. Perhaps this was one of the manifestations of what the Christian faith considered resurrection.

⸻

As Christine left what had been Bertrand's home, she felt that she had met the embodiment of true love. She knew that she would come back to the Peak very soon. Christine was now sure that Bertrand Wilmington had not committed suicide. Somebody who had decided to turn the page of his successful career to go to Sidney to research gender and equality was a man who had a life ahead of him.

Christine joined Victoria at her apartment. They both needed to feel at home that night.

29

VICTORIA WAS A MASTER AT PREPARING DIM SUM MEALS. SHE HAD opened a bottle of Brunello Del Montalcino, her favorite Italian wine. She thought its joyfulness would suit them both.

Christine and Victoria agreed that the answer lay at BHS and that a criminal investigation was becoming unavoidable. That didn't mean that the person responsible was an BHS employee, however. The Chongqing lead could not be ignored. There weren't many suspects, but the complexity of their relationships made it difficult for Victoria and Christine to point to a single person. More importantly, how would the police be able to find proof of the murder? Would they even be willing to reopen the inquiry?

The detectives needed documentation from the Wilmingtons of Bertrand's enrollment at the University of Sydney and his travel plans. That was the most persuasive evidence that the death was a homicide.

Christine and Victoria were also inclined to look more closely at Henry Chang's behavior. After all, he had lied to Victoria, and the fact that he oversaw Bertrand's clients and trades certainly gave him ample motive. One piece of the puzzle was essential: why had David Chen input proprietary trades into Bertrand's book? This was most unusual, and, at the same time, David knew he would be picked up by the BHS system and immediately investigated by the audit and compliance department. The trades would have been returned to the proprietary desk the next day. David must have known that the audit department had been zeroing in on Bertrand.

As they considered the alternatives, Victoria's phone rang. It was Henry Chang. His voice seemed strange, and she could hear he was out of breath and in a panic.

"I need to see you immediately."

"What happened?"

"I just left Harvey Lee's office. They went through all of my e-mails and trades while I was not authorized to go to the office. They clearly see me as a suspect. I don't know what Harvey heard in Shanghai. He would not even tell me whom he met!"

"Have you been drinking?"

"Yes, I probably drank a bit too much, but I can reason and understand the situation. I am here in Kowloon, not far from your apartment. Could I come up?"

"You must be kidding, Henry! The only place where I'll meet you is the office. Are you in danger?"

"Professionally, yes, but not physically."

"What if the perpetrators were from Chongqing, and they arranged Bertrand's 'suicide'?" Victoria asked.

"Do you believe that's possible?" Henry gasped.

"I can't exclude anything. Did you convince them that you would take care of Bertrand, as they asked you?"

"Probably not. I certainly never said anything like that."

"Have you talked to Diana today?"

"Yes, I saw her at the bar of the Mandarin Oriental. She grilled me."

"Did you manage to explain to her what happened?"

"Yes, but there are still elements that I am not willing to tell her."

Victoria smiled. Diana was tough and wouldn't let him go until she knew everything. She had invited Henry nicely and probably let him have a few drinks. Victoria had seen Diana in action at the fraud department. When she was interrogating, she was an iron lady and could make anybody confess. It was Diana's turn to claw back at Henry, and she would certainly have no compassion for him, whatever consequences he faced.

"What was Diana interested in?"

"The Oriental Real Estate IPO. She discovered that I was part of the management team for the transaction. Some shares were misallocated to a broker-dealer, Oriental Finance, and they made some profit on it."

"Did she figure out whether you benefited from the scam?"

"Yes, she did, and she's now threatening to reopen that investigation and get me indicted and jailed. I'm frightened."

"Well, you know, she is entitled to lock you up for seventy-two hours without explanation. In the hands of the fraud department, that's a long time. Very few people resist this kind of pressure without sleep."

"Am I still your client, Victoria?!"

"Yes, you are, but you also lied to us. So now I have to second-guess everything you tell me. Did you tell Harvey Lee everything?"

"Yes, I did. But I'm not sure he trusts me enough to take what I told him at face value."

"You can understand that, can't you? I'll see you at my office tomorrow morning at eight. I'm not sure how safe you are. Find a room somewhere. Do not sleep in your apartment. At this stage, the stakes are so high that anything can happen."

"If they got Bertrand, I'm probably next in line. That's a scary thought. Thank you for the warning."

⸺

Christine had listened to the conversation in silence. Not being privy to the details of the investigation, she couldn't understand what was really at stake, but she could recognize the desperation and fear in Henry's voice.

Victoria had been right to refuse to meet him now. Any conversation with a drunken man had no value, and he could have been threatening (or worse). The only way Victoria could help Henry as a client was to be completely professional and to ignore everything she knew on the private side.

"This is so confusing," Victoria said. "Henry looks like a victim, but guys like him are paper tigers. They act as if they're the masters of the universe and terrorize their fellow traders, but once they're the focus of an investigation, they become incredibly scared. That's where Henry is now."

The friends took solace in their dinner. Christine and Victoria again discussed the details of the visit with the Wilmingtons, including Bertrand's plan to go to Sydney. Victoria immediately understood the importance of the information.

"That is crucial. It makes the suicide theory difficult to maintain. It might allow us to get the police to reopen the case. I'll inform Diana Yu tomorrow."

After Christine had left, Victoria called one of her colleagues in the Mainland and asked him if he could investigate the questions Harvey Lee had raised. They also had a long discussion about the intelligence he had on the mayor's entourage. While it was nothing conclusive, it cast a grim light on financial practices in one of the most shining Chinese cities.

Victoria wondered whether the assault she had suffered might have been ordered by Chongqing.

30

Olivia Shuler had become so upset by her boss's behavior
that she contacted Victoria Leung to talk about a meeting that had
taken place before Bertrand's death. Louis Cheung had told Olivia
that Victoria was leading the investigation. It would have been difficult to talk candidly at the office, so Olivia called from home. Victoria
picked up the call even though it was very early.

"Hello? This is Olivia Shuler, David Chen's assistant at BHS. Is
this Victoria Leung?"

"Yes. Nice talking to you. You're calling bright and early."

"Exactly. I need to talk to you about a meeting that took place a
couple of days prior to Bertrand Wilmington's death. Could we meet
somewhere?"

"Where are you at the moment?"

"In Kowloon."

"Let's meet at the Regent. Would that work for you?"

"Absolutely. In fifteen minutes?"

Fifteen minutes later, Victoria was seated at the Regent when
Olivia walked in. Olivia Shuler had all the attributes of a senior professional and a lady. She had earned a law degree at the University
of Geneva: when she met her husband, they decided to make his

UNICEF role the priority. Since then, she had found a new professional challenge in all the places where he had been stationed. She
had worked as a nurse in a children's hospital and as the organizer of
an NGO. When they arrived in Hong Kong, Olivia was offered her
current position.

Olivia told Victoria about the series of recent events with David
Chen. During the few days that preceded Bertrand Wilmington's death,
Olivia had noticed a few anomalies in David's behavior. He had also,
unusually overruled restrictions on trades that the proprietary desk had
sent him in order to send them directly to Bertrand's client accounts.

Olivia had asked him about this and was faced with an irate boss.

"Can you for once understand that this is none of your business?"
David had shouted. "You are an assistant; you cannot even compre-
hend the world I am operating in or the rules of the game. You are
here at my discretion. If you start meddling, I will fire you. Do you
understand? I have my deals with each of the main traders, and they
need to be respected."

"Mary Li, the head of audit, called me," Olivia had responded.

"That bitch had better stay at her desk if she wants to keep her job."

"She's on her way here with somebody from compliance. It's about
the proprietary account."

"I won't see them," David had growled.

"Are you sure you have the choice?"

"I always have a choice. Don't get involved for your own sake. Is
that clear?"

"It is perfectly clear, but they're in your meeting room." Olivia had
said. "They expect to talk to you."

"Tell them I have to run to a meeting."

Olivia explained to Victoria that she had then left and delivered
the message to his visitors. They stood up and went straight to David
Chen's office. Olivia understood perfectly that the matter was absolutely critical and connected to the unusual trades he had authorized.
Olivia stood by the door and listened carefully.

"Didn't Olivia tell you I had a meeting?" David Chen had said when the visitors came in.

"Yes, she did," Mary Li had replied. "But you also made some fraudulent proprietary trades. Which one is more important?"

Another man had then stepped forward. "I am Greg Simpson. I run the compliance department. This meeting cannot be further delayed."

Gregory Simpson, a newcomer to Hong Kong, was in charge of compliance for the fixed-income department, overseen by Harvey Lee. He was the first line of fire when the front or back office did not respect rules and regulations. Harvey had brought him in from London to support the inquiry into the actions in the trading room. He took his business seriously and was more of a problem solver than an inquisitor. However, when manipulations or irregularities arose, he was impossible to circumvent. Gregory zeroed in on issues like an eagle and got to the bottom of them quickly. David's attitude was exactly what he despised the most: a businessperson who surrounded himself with systemic fear in order to avoid having to comply with rules and regulations.

Olivia continued recounting the story. David Chen stood, grabbed his jacket, and tried to push Mary Li out of his way. Gregory Simpson stopped him.

"I am going to my meeting. You have no authority to stop me," David had barked.

Mary Li knew guys like him: they acted proud and arrogant, but inside they were deeply insecure. His anger was a manifestation of his panic. But Mary had no fear, and the presence of a compliance colleague was enough of a message for David to take the visit seriously. But, David believed he was invincible. He continued to the door.

"If you don't speak to us now, your next meeting will be with Harvey Lee and the head of the enforcement division of the SFC," Mary had said sternly. "Either you deal with us, or you deal with the authorities."

David went back to his desk.

"Why did you dump proprietary positions on client accounts?"

"John Highbridge asked me to," David had responded.

"Why would he do that? You know nobody is allowed to do that. It is absolutely prohibited."

"I just wanted to help. You can ask him."

Mary seized the opportunity. "Ask John to join us, Olivia."

David was sweating. Mary and Greg wouldn't let him go until they had gotten the information they had come for.

John Highbridge had joined the meeting, and Greg explained why he and Mary were there.

"I have to reduce my positions, Greg," John had said defensively. "I am beyond the new limits in derivatives, and after the London Whale scandal at JP Morgan, London did a full survey of our own principal derivative positions and instructed us to liquidate them intelligently but quickly, as they put it, which is the buzzword for not dumping but not waiting."

"That doesn't mean you could send them directly to a client's account," Greg had interjected.

"I talked about it with David, and he told me he might have a few ideas. The next thing I saw was this transfer of HK$50 million. I assumed it had been done with Bertrand Wilmington and Henry Chang's agreement. Are you telling me that the position was transferred to a Chinese fund without the agreement of Bertrand and his client?"

"That's exactly what it looks like," Greg had responded.

David was now in the eye of the storm. "I did mention it to Bertrand, and he told me he was okay with it," David added.

"Why do you think he came to me to ask if I could audit that trade?" Mary had said. "It appeared on his screen by surprise."

"Do you know where the money went?" Greg had asked.

"I don't remember."

"Let me refresh your memory: the Chongqing Hedge Fund."

"Holy shit . . ."

"Yes. Henry is now in Shanghai to explain what happened."

"Why Shanghai?"

"He was summoned by the fund managers."

"This is really bad."

"Yes, and we expect the CSRC to realize what happened very quickly. You have some explaining to do David."

Olivia then explained that Bertrand Wilmington was asked to join the meeting. When he came in, Olivia recalled seeing fear in his eyes. They had already had some rough times with David. However, the presence of personnel from audit, compliance, and proprietary trading was reassuring.

"Bertrand," Mary had said, "when you came to see me yesterday, you were worried about the fact that a HK$50 million derivatives position had been transferred to one of your clients' accounts directly from 1130-01 without your knowledge."

"That's indeed what I noticed, and I wanted to be sure everything was regular. I couldn't understand what was going on," Bertrand had replied.

David leapt from his chair. "You know I talked to you about it! I told you I was helping John Highbridge reduce his position."

"You did, David, but not until I came to your office to ask for an explanation—*after* the trade was executed. You *never* asked me whether my client was willing to buy that position."

"You are a chicken-shit liar, Bertrand! You knew everything, and now that compliance and audit are present, you're backing off. You are so pathetic!" David had screamed.

"Hey!" John Highbridge had intervened. "This is not the way to find out what happened. I'm also a part of this. Bertrand, are you telling us that the position appeared on your screen straight from 1130-01 without your consent?"

"Exactly."

"Get out of my room!" David had shouted.

"Stop it, David," Gregory had said. "You can yell as much as you want, but that won't undo the fact that you thought you were doing John a favor by dumping the position. Why did you do it?"

"You can't prove I did anything," David had barked.

"Only your computer with your personal key can deactivate the blocking of such transactions," Gregory had explained. "Unless you gave your personal key to somebody, nobody but you could have done it. We saw the sequence: our systems told you that this was not authorized. But you overruled it, a privilege that only you can exercise when there is a documented explanation to do so. There is no documentation in this case."

David had sat in silence for a moment before responding. "You're right. I forgot about the documentation."

"That's not the point, David. Why did you do it?" Greg had asked again.

Olivia had interrupted at that moment: "I believe that there are some other elements to this, particularly the relationship between David and Bertrand."

"What do you mean?" Gregory had asked.

"Shut up, Olivia! That concerns my private life! You are not allowed to disclose it," David had screamed.

"This is totally irregular," Mary had agreed. "The meeting is adjourned. We will be back to you soon."

Victoria sat staring at Olivia, taking in all the details. She saw the picture more fully as she listened to Olivia's report, which clearly put the Chongqing Hedge Fund at the center of the inquiry but also made David's role even more opaque.

"Thank you very much, Olivia. This is so helpful. The problem is becoming so much more complex, and it will be tough to close it in a few days. I assume you reported back to Mary."

"What happened since the death of Bertrand Wilmington?" asked Olivia.

Her distress was obvious. She knew Bertrand as a decent man while his boss was a bully who did not respect the rules. She had also read suspicious e-mails in his personal inbox.

"I cannot tell you much, Olivia. All I can say is that I do not believe that Bertrand committed suicide. He was about to leave BHS for Australia."

31

DAVID CHEN HAD LEFT HONG KONG FOR HIS HOLIDAY IN BALI THE day after Bertrand Wilmington's death, as planned, as if nothing had happened. He had told Olivia that he saw no reason not to spend time with his wife and kids. He would call her every day.

On his first daily call to Olivia, David had asked her to go to his computer. She had the access code to his e-mails, and he told her to delete all his personal e-mail exchanges with Bertrand Wilmington.

Olivia knew he was asking her to destroy evidence, and since Victoria had told her that Bertrand might have been murdered, her legal background immediately mobilized her instincts.

"Why don't you use your VPN and do it yourself?"

"Because I'm on vacation and it would look suspicious. If you do it, it will be your mistake. Got it?"

"I get that you want me to illegally delete e-mails at the risk of losing my job because you are not willing to assume responsibility for your own actions. Anyway, I'll do it after lunch. Don't count on me to cover for you, though. If something goes wrong, I will tell the truth."

Olivia had immediately called Mary Li and Gregory Simpson and asked them for advice. Mary had told her to go out for lunch, as she had told David she would. Within an hour, the entire hard disk and e-mail system on David's computer were duplicated to the audit department system. When Olivia had come back to the office, she saw that the personal e-mails had been cleaned out. It was obvious what had happened.

That afternoon, David had called Olivia again. "I see that the e-mails have been deleted."

"Yes, I did what you told me to do."

"Thank you for being loyal to me, Olivia. I will reward you for that when I come back. Sorry for my rudeness."

"I don't mind the rudeness as long as what we do is legal. I am a lawyer by training, as you know." Olivia had recognized his usual manipulative tone and ignored it. "Enjoy the beach."

Olivia was deeply worried by the whole situation, but knew she had done the right thing. What would happen next was between David and the firm. She knew the contents of those e-mails and was sure they would incriminate her boss.

32

The place Diana and Victoria had chosen was just right for them. They had left the city center for Wan Chai and were sitting at the Grand Hyatt Hotel in the Teppan room of the Kaetsu Japanese restaurant for sushi. They enjoyed the light spring breeze on the modern terrace overlooking the bay. It was the time of year for dresses. Nobody watching them chatting would believe they were a senior detective and a member of the financial fraud department of the Hong Kong Police Force. They looked like any two young women enjoying a break.

"What can you tell me?" Diana asked.

"Henry Chang is in deep trouble. He was in the trading room the night of Bertrand Wilmington's death, which we have reason to believe might have been a homicide."

"Wow. Why is that?"

"Bertrand had decided to leave BHS for Sydney," Victoria said.

"Yes, we figured that out, but it didn't seem to be more than a visit with family," Diana replied.

"We thought that too, until my colleague Christine Freed talked to his parents and found out that he was going to resign the next day and had accepted an offer from a research program on gender and equality at the University of Sydney. A man who has decided to change his life for the better does not commit suicide."

"If you can produce the evidence tonight, I would like to inform my colleagues," Diana admitted. "We'll probably conclude that these new facts warrant the reopening of the case as a possible murder case. I feel so bad, Victoria. This is not the Henry I know. It's devastating."

Victoria held her friend's hand tightly. She knew how much it hurt. After a few minutes, the waiter brought their salads, and as they ate, Diana asked:

"How's your investigation going?"

"In the last few days, it's taken an unexpected turn. Commissioner Chu's counterpart at the Shanghai police alerted him to some implications of Bertrand Wilmington's death in Mainland China."

"How does that affect Henry?" interjected Diana.

"Henry was the account manager for all fixed-income activities of China's official agencies. He went to see his clients in Shanghai the day before Bertrand's death. The clients were arrested at the airport after they left the meeting with Henry."

"The Chinese authorities will never tell us everything they know. But neither will we. Are they interfering with the inquiry?"

"No, but what we have learned could indicate that the Chongqing gang could have had a vested interest in killing Bertrand," answered Victoria.

"Why?"

"He discovered that the account he was dealing with was a phantom account that was benefitting the fund managers and their friends."

"I'm sure the Chongqing gang didn't like that."

"The question is whether they might have tried to eliminate Bertrand to avoid being discovered by the anticorruption team that was investigating their finances."

"That would give this whole inquiry a totally different dimension: should the management of a municipality have eliminated a banker in

Hong Kong, the whole issue of the independence of the Hong Kong capital markets would be implicated."

"The Shanghai police gave us two weeks to sort out the case and hope it will remain confined to Hong Kong. Otherwise, they will have to step in. The CSRC is also talking about securities fraud with the SFC."

"That is consistent with what I heard."

The complexity of the financial ramifications of the case made it essential for Pegasus to cooperate with the police. In some cases—like murder—the stakes were so high that only cooperation made it possible to assemble the puzzle.

"How are you coping, Victoria?"

"I'm okay, I guess. All my energies are focused on this investigation. I'll need some rest after it's resolved."

"Those of us who know you at the police force made the connection with the Macau restaurant attack. You didn't tell me about it."

"I didn't want to embarrass you, since I'd rather not see the police force involved in my case. I hope you understand my position."

"You should have talked to me, although I perfectly understand your reasoning. But some of us do know."

Victoria had pushed the assault far back in her brain, but with one word, her friend had brought it to the fore. It was painful but also good to talk.

"What I saw there was so much hatred from the aggressors," Victoria said. "They were so mean. I don't understand why courts continue to treat rape differently from other types of aggression. If a man is bullied, he isn't asked how he was dressed, whether he was drunk, or whether he invited the punches."

"We see it all the time. When women are raped, we have to justify that we weren't guilty of any provocation. This is absolutely intolerable. Will you remain silent?"

"No. If the police decide to prosecute the three men, I would be willing to testify in court, and I'll do anything I can to have them sent to jail. Did you know that Louis Cheung has been questioned by the police?"

"Yes."

"How has he been treated?"

"Pretty badly; the police officers humiliated him because he's gay. But he wanted to make a public case of the protection that is granted to antigay activities like this. When the criminal division finds out that you're willing to testify, we'll do what we can to ensure they behave decently."

"That makes me feel so good. I'll contact Louis. This could be a unique opportunity to influence the way cases like this are handled. You made my day, Diana."

33

On her way back to the office, Victoria went through the shopping malls that populated Hong Kong's underground galleries and stopped at the Prince's Building. She went to the third floor, where the main fashion houses were displaying their beautiful summer collections. This summer would be bright with pastel colors. J. Crew had an incredible collection of tops and shorts. Victoria liked a green pastel tank top and white shorts and tried them on. She was ready to feel like a summer woman again. She looked at herself in the mirror: she didn't so much like the image of herself, but the outfit was certainly flattering and to her taste. She bought it.

Carrying her shopping bag, she felt lighter as she entered the office. Judy told her the boss was waiting to talk to her.

"I like that smile," Sir Francis said. "In the mess we're in, it is certainly refreshing. Any good news I should know?"

"No. I just went shopping after my lunch with Diana. I bought a summer outfit and felt like a woman again."

"What did you hear from Diana?" Sir Francis asked.

"As expected, the Shanghai police have contacted the Hong Kong Police Force, and the CSRC has contacted the SFC."

"Did you give Diana a heads up about our investigation?"

"I told her that we believe it is a homicide case and why. She will certainly inform Commissioner Chu, who will not be surprised by our analysis when he attends the meeting tomorrow. Surprises with the police are not your friends," Victoria added.

"So true. You obviously know how to handle them. On my side, I talked to Harvey Lee. He informed the SFC of the irregular trading. The commission will launch an inquiry and visit BHS tomorrow. They want to understand what happened, and Harvey will discuss some measures BHS intends to implement."

"Any news about David Chen?" Victoria asked.

"He's on vacation, believe it or not. His secretary came forward with information on the trades that were sent to Bertrand Wilmington. She's been working closely with the audit department. Apparently David attempted to destroy some evidence. He'll be back tonight. By tomorrow, we'll have more information."

"Harvey Lee told Henry Chang not to come to the office until Monday, and he gave them the name of his lawyer for future contact about the investigation," Victoria said. "The lawyer called Harvey almost immediately to explain what he had told the SFC and the police, and he ensured Harvey that BHS could rely on him to provide as much evidence as necessary. BHS believes that Henry and David colluded in altering the account number. They're still incredulous about the possibility that they might have pushed Bertrand to his death, but they're looking at that possibility seriously now."

Would Henry be able to extricate himself from this situation? Both Sir Francis and Victoria asked themselves the same question. There was no way he would escape unscathed, they thought.

"It must have been tough for Henry to make the decision to cooperate," Victoria continued. "He'll be exposed and vilified, but he owes it to Bertrand. No matter what comes from the investigation, if he had acted courageously, he could have prevented these dramatic events."

"I agree. As you know better than others, the silence in trading rooms is dogmatically enforced. Henry will need to be physically protected by the police for some time. Too many people might want him eliminated. However, we are not sure yet about his role in Bertrand's death. He hasn't been forthcoming about it."

"I advised him to stay in a hotel," Victoria said. "He might need to go back to London. He has a superb apartment in South Kensington. He won't be safe in Hong Kong once he's testified. Even if Henry himself gets some jail time, any of his colleagues who are arraigned will never forgive him. He might even have to leave the financial services industry altogether."

"That's likely," Sir Francis agreed. "He's lucky enough to have the financial means to rebuild himself."

Henry could live anywhere. His father had asked him to take over the family shipping business. This might be the right moment for him to answer the family call. He had been considering that option for a while.

"I also heard that Louis Cheung reported the assault," Victoria added, "and that the police have decided to prosecute the three perpetrators. That was courageous of Louis. He wants to make a case against the antigay crimes in Hong Kong. I'll tell him that I'll testify at the trial and support his case. It's the least I could do."

After the conversation, Victoria returned to her office to find several messages on her desk. Without looking any further, she called Louis.

"Louis, it's Victoria."

"Good to hear your voice."

"I understand from Diana that you reported the assault at the Macau restaurant. That was very brave of you."

"Thank you. I didn't mention you."

"The police know I was involved anyway. How did they treat you?"

"I got the usual humiliating comments that straight men make about gay people. They are just ignorant. I recorded the interrogation. Even though the recording won't be accepted as a testimony, it will probably force the police to treat victims as victims, not perpetrators.

Interestingly, when they understood you had also been assaulted, they became much more careful."

"Absolutely. I wanted to tell you that I've decided to testify if this comes to trial. I had reasons not to report this since the police were already involved. I feel strongly that the three men should face jail time. Otherwise, these crimes will continue unpunished."

Louis smiled. "That is such great news, Victoria. Your testimony will carry so much weight in court."

"Louis, I want to update you on the case. We have now concluded that Bertrand Wilmington's death was a homicide. The police will probably announce tonight that they're reopening the inquiry for criminal charges. I cannot tell you how happy I am at that conclusion."

"I'm sure you played a critical role in this, Victoria. It is such a huge relief. I never lost faith in Bertrand. Did you know he would have moved to Australia if he had not been killed? We were planning to get married there."

"Yes, I do. We heard it from his parents."

"I was supposed to take over a hotel in Sydney this fall, but you'll get my testimony on this. Who could have killed Bertrand?" Louis asked.

"We're not short of suspects, and the ties back to China make the case even more opaque."

"Why would Mainland be involved?"

"Bertrand was trading with Mainland investors and might have discovered some fraud that the managers didn't like."

"Could they have killed Bertrand?" Louis shuddered.

Even through the phone, Victoria could hear that he was overwhelmed by emotion. He thanked her quietly and hung up. She could only imagine what this meant for him and his attachment to Bertrand. She had also been moved by the conversation. What a nice couple they must have been and what a future they could have had. It was time for justice.

Sir Francis called Victoria on the intercom. "Your lunch with

Diana Yu did the job. I got a call from Harvey. Commissioner Chu had just called him. HKPF wants to talk about the result of your investigation of Bertrand Wilmington's death at tonight's meeting. When you confirm what Bertrand's parents told us, they will announce the reopening of the investigation. They'll conduct the autopsy tomorrow morning."

"Thank you, Francis. This is great news."

"Congratulations, Victoria."

She hung up. It was huge to get a case reopened. She thought of Bertrand Wilmington, his parents, and Louis Cheung. Judy Wang brought her some green tea and a tissue.

"I'm so proud of you," Judy said. "You cannot imagine what it means for so many of us to know that there are women who can fight a battle against violence that sometimes seems so hopeless."

"Thank you. It means a lot. Please ask Christine to join us."

Christine came over immediately.

"The police will reopen the inquiry on Bertrand Wilmington's death," Victoria said. "It will be announced tonight."

"This is such wonderful news," Christine cried.

"I want you to inform his parents. Would you call them, please?"

Christine tried to guess the impact the news would have. It would be a relief for them to know that their child might not have committed suicide, which was the worst thing parents could face; it destroyed a vital part of themselves. However, Bertrand's homicide would raise other questions.

"I'd like to tell them face-to-face," Christine said. "I believe that's the best way to relay this news. It will come as a shock, and I'd like to stay until the news breaks on television. They might need practical advice."

Victoria agreed. "You are so right, Christine. Please go there quickly."

34

THE OFFICES OF THE HONG KONG SECURITIES AND FINANCE Commission were located on the thirty-fifth floor of a modern building in Queen's Road Central. It was a prime location between the Court of Appeals, the central government offices, and the Bank of China headquarters. The view from the boardroom was spectacular, and, on this spring day, the sunset over the bay cast the warm light that photographers most prized for landscape photos.

Sir Francis, Laura Woo, and Victoria were the first to enter the room, and Victoria's blue dress added deep color to it. She had been in the same room before for the Kwok brother's case and was struck again by the rather sober atmosphere that the long rosewood table created. At every seat was a white mug inscribed with "Informed investors Quality markets!"

The back door opened and Ian Adler, the Commission's CEO, entered the room. He was a British lawyer who had worked with Herbert Smith LLP, where he was the head of operations in Asia, until 2011. Adler enjoyed the respect of his peers and had personal relationships with Sir Francis, Harvey Lee, and Laura Woo, who had been the CEO of the Commission when Adler worked on securities issues for Hong Kong clients. Adler was also respected in China for designing venerated rules and policies, especially for dual filings. A tall and elegantly dressed man, he projected a mix of severity and confidence.

He had succeeded Martin Wheatley when Wheatley had returned to London to be the CEO of the UK's Financial Services Authority. Wheatley had immediately been thrown into the LIBOR scandal in the City of London.

John Wilcox, Harvey Lee, and their colleagues introduced themselves, followed by Hong Kong Police Force Commissioner Liu Chu and the head of the fraud department, Diana Yu.

The atmosphere was quiet and grave. This case would influence Hong Kong's reputation as a global financial center and its standing in the world capital markets.

Commissioner Chu opened the discussion: "We are here to find out what implications the reopening of the Bertrand Wilmington case might have. However, before we get there, I'd like to hear from Pegasus about its reasons for believing the death to be a crime."

With his distinctive soft-spoken authority, Sir Francis thanked the commissioner for inviting them to the meeting and indicated that the investigation began at a client's request to investigate the circumstances surrounding Bertrand Wilmington's death. He then gave the floor to Victoria Leung.

Although her heart raced, Victoria spoke assertively. "In the course of our investigation, we met with Bertrand Wilmington's friends and family to gain the necessary clarity. What we learned contradicted the idea that Bertrand was a depressed and burned-out man.

"For a few months, Bertrand had looked into the possibility of leaving Hong Kong with his partner, Louis Cheung. What he left behind was not a suicide note. He was talking about leaving the firm and the city.

"He was scheduled to depart a week after his death, and he had already sent his personal belongings to there. Both Louis and Bertrand's parents informed us that Bertrand was going to resign from BHS the next Monday. He had received a grant from the University of

Sydney's Department of Gender and Culture, which we confirmed with the University of Sydney's provost. He was stunned by the news and could not understand how such an enthusiastic and talented man could be the same one who jumped from the twenty-second floor of BHS's offices."

"Are you talking about the same Louis Cheung who was assaulted by that gang of antigay men?" Commissioner Chu asked.

"Indeed," Victoria said. "The combination of all of these factors makes the suicide conclusion difficult to sustain."

"So there is more to this than a possible securities trading problem? You've indicated that he was gay, so gender conflicts might have played a role here."

"Yes, Commissioner Chu."

"I understand from the inquiry into the assault that one of the aggressors was from BHS and that a former member of our police fraud office had also been sexually assaulted as she was having dinner with Louis. Could it be . . . ?"

A heavy silence followed. It was clear why the commissioner hadn't finished the sentence.

"Yes, I was the second person attacked, Commissioner Chu."

"Now I understand why you're called the Flying Dragon," the Commissioner said. "Let's have a ten-minute break. I need to consult my colleagues in the criminal department."

Diana and Victoria headed for the restroom. The rest of the attendees were silent.

With Victoria and Diana out of the room, Harvey Lee spoke first. "The day after the attack, Victoria took incredible personal risks to find the truth. And she paid the price. That is nothing short of remarkable."

"We gave her as much support as we could," Laura Woo said. "Her inner strength is impressive. It seems that the target of the attack was

Louis Cheung, and that the men assumed Victoria was a lesbian and attacked her for that reason. It is absolutely despicable."

Diana's colleague, William Young, the head of the criminal department, then entered the room.

"Mr. Young has confirmed that the inquiry into Bertrand Wilmington's death is now a homicide investigation," Commissioner Chu said. "That puts additional pressure on all of us, but we're used to such cases and will take all necessary precautions. The autopsy will take place tomorrow, and we'll make a public statement. The press release will be issued tomorrow morning. We will have to inform the Department of Justice, and a district attorney will run the investigation."

As the meeting closed, all participants were coming to grips with the implications of this new information. This was no longer just a question of money. Somebody had been murdered.

35

CHRISTINE FREED APPROACHED THE WILMINGTONS' APARTMENT. She was glad that she had volunteered to visit them about the change in the status of the investigation, and she had called them to make sure they were prepared to meet her. She hoped that they would be relieved by the turn of events despite the inevitable consequences it would have on their lives.

Christopher Wilmington waited for Christine at the building's entrance, and he let her in with a warm handshake. Up at the apartment, Catherine Wilmington greeted her with a hug. As they entered the living room, a man was there sitting in an armchair. He stood.

"I am Louis Cheung, Bertrand's friend. I was here when you called, and Mr. and Mrs. Wilmington asked me to stay. I gather you are a colleague of Victoria Leung at Pegasus."

"I am indeed. As we speak, she is attending a meeting with the authorities and BHS. How are you holding up?" Christine gestured to his broken arm.

"The attackers broke my arm. How is Victoria coping? I haven't seen her since we had dinner at the Macau restaurant. Was she hurt?"

"Only superficially, but the shock has been tough for her to overcome, as I am sure it has been for you."

Catherine brought in tea, and everyone sat down.

"The meeting Victoria is attending includes the police commis-sioner," Christine explained. "Diana Yu, the head of the financial fraud department, whom Louis might have heard about, briefed the Commissioner on the relevant events. She had succeeded Victoria in her previous job at the fraud department."

"What was the meeting about?" Louis asked.

"Victoria presented the information you all provided that sug-gests that Bertrand's death was not a suicide. On that basis, the police have reopened the case as a homicide investigation."

Christine remained silent as they absorbed the information. Christopher put his head in his hands and sobbed. Catherine sat like a statue as tears rolled down her cheeks.

Louis was astounded but managed to speak. "I told Victoria that suicide was totally impossible. I'm as happy as I am terrified by the news. Who could have wanted to kill Bertrand? Why? It's unbeliev-able. Do you know anything else?"

"The police will start their investigation," Christine continued, "and the Department of Justice will immediately designate a public prosecutor to handle the case."

Still incredulous, Christopher went to the balcony for some fresh air. His wife joined him. They digested the importance of the devel-opment and what it meant for them.

When they came back inside, Catherine spoke. "We are relieved, Christine. It had been an ordeal to imagine what could have led Bertrand to commit suicide. We spent days and nights trying to un-derstand his motives."

"We tortured ourselves, wondering if there was anything we could have done to prevent his suicide," Christopher added. "This nightmare is finally over. We can now face a different reality where our son is a victim and start mourning him. Thank you."

Louis burst into tears, and Catherine comforted him. How could one handle such a terrible loss?

"Our wounds will heal, but nothing will ever replace what we've lost," Catherine said.

Christopher Wilmington slowly regained his ability to reason. "What will be expected of us?" he asked. "I've always hated publicity, and this will become a public matter. This is tough enough even without the aggravation of the media."

"You're right, Christopher. A criminal investigation will soon be announced, and the media will probably give the case a fair amount of visibility," Christine said. "You can expect journalists to locate you and maybe camp out in front of your apartment to get interviews."

"What do you think we should we do?"

"Do you have friends in Hong Kong you could stay with?"

"My sister lives around here," Catherine said. "She has been extraordinarily supportive and could certainly accommodate us. How long do you think this will last?"

"I don't think the investigation will take more than a week. We can help make sure that the police take your deposition early. Once that's done, you can go wherever you'd like. If you can, I suggest that you leave the country to avoid the overwhelming media coverage and reactions from friends, however well-intentioned they are."

"We'll think about it and make plans as soon as we can," Christopher said. "We have a house in Surrey, and spring is a good time to go to England. Thank you for your advice."

Once those basics had been discussed, there was no reason for Christine to stay any longer. She stood up and hugged everyone goodbye. The truth is a powerful healing force.

She called Victoria to inform her of the Wilmingtons' plans.

36

WHEN THE MEMBERS OF THE POLICE DEPARTMENT LEFT THE MEETing, the tone changed. Everybody around the table knew each other very well, and many had held the same or similar positions. They shared the same professionalism, knew the complexities of securities regulation, and often enough had been on panels addressing some of the difficulties of implementing those rules, which were well-intentioned but often far from the realities of day-to-day trading.

Chairman Adler spoke next. "Harvey, I understand that this affects some of your internal operations and some that fall under the SFC's purview. I also got a phone call from CSRC Chairman James Liu, who informed me that you've discussed the Chongqing Hedge Fund account. As you know, Beijing closely follows anything affecting the Chongqing municipality, and the CSRC is giving us two weeks to sort out the problem. After that they will have to step into the inquiry directly. It's a challenge, but the last thing we want is a direct Beijing inquiry into Hong Kong financial matters."

"Yes," Harvey nodded, "that is why I immediately flew to Shanghai. I am aware of the two-week hold. Our inquiry should be finalized by then. With the agreement of the authorities, we kept the originals of our commitments with the fund in London. We only retain copies here. The two signatories of the copies are Henry Chang and David Chen. Our own forensic investigation came to the conclusion that the account documents had been altered. We received a fraudulent account number and did not realize it immediately because the account numbers appear without hyphens, periods, and commas, when viewed electronically. Victoria led us in the right direction."

"What happened with the Chongqing managers?" Chairman Adler asked.

"The Shanghai police, under the instructions of the CSRC, arrested the asset managers who organized the fraud as they boarded their plane back to Chongqing."

"This is outside of our jurisdiction, but we need to figure out if there was anything that contributed to the fraud on our side," Chairman Adler said.

"Actually, it might not be outside Hong Kong's jurisdiction," Victoria said. "I have contacted my colleagues in China. One of them did work at the Chongqing municipality and might be able to inform us of its possible involvement in Bertrand's homicide."

"I alluded to that theory when I met the CSRC in Shanghai," Harvey said. "They flatly denied that anything could have come from them. I do not know whether they will investigate it any further. What did you learn from your colleague, Victoria?"

Victoria explained. "The municipality's staff was disbanded when the mayor was arrested. It is extremely difficult to track them down. However, behind the three fund managers, there are a few political appointees. The risk is therefore far from being nil. What mitigates it, however, is that they would need to have inside accomplices at BHS."

"We will need to come to the BHS offices to audit the situation," Chairman Adler said.

"You are most welcome to send your audit executives tomorrow to the bank, Harvey said. "We will share everything we know. Hopefully our observations will be the same."

"Perfect. Let's focus on the proprietary trading side of the issue, the securities-regulation infringement," Chairman Adler suggested.

"Yes. Based on the conversation Bertrand had with our audit department two days before his death, it seems that the questionable trades were coming from the back office and not from the proprietary trading desk. That office is run by David Chen. He will be here tomorrow. However, David's secretary informed us of his attempts to delete several personal e-mails to Bertrand Wilmington. This is where the sexual harassment issue and the regulatory issue cross. As soon as we meet David and understand what he has to say, we will come back to you. It should not take more than twenty-four hours."

Harvey Lee's explanation was as sober and as clear as it could have been for a pretty messy situation. By disclosing everything BHS knew at this stage, Harvey had strengthened the goodwill between the bank and the SFC.

Sir Francis then cut in to explain Henry Chang's role in the investigation thus far.

"Henry is no longer allowed to operate until we come to the final conclusion," Harvey Lee said when Sir Francis finished speaking. "The same applies to David Chen."

Victoria then explained how Henry had withheld information from her during the investigation and the difficulty in getting him provide *all* relevant information. "In the context of a criminal inquiry, we expect him to come forward and cooperate both with the police and with BHS. I assume that his attorney reached out to you. He remains affected by Bertrand's death and wanted us to get to the bottom of it. As someone immersed in the management of trading rooms, he will now have to break the conspiracy of silence that bonds the trading world."

Chairman Adler and Harvey Lee asked Laura Woo to act as an advisor on the matter, since she was an independent party. She agreed, pending confirmation that doing so would not be a conflict of interest.

The meeting then wrapped up, and Sir Francis invited Laura Woo and Victoria to join him at his club for a working dinner.

At dinner, they spent time reviewing all aspects of the developments of the day. Victoria discussed Christine's conversation with Bertrand's parents and asked if she could call Diana to ensure that, if the police needed to interrogate the Wilmingtons, they would do so early and limit the time they would need to stay in Hong Kong. She explained that they would retreat for a while with Mrs. Wilmington's sister until they could go to their country house in Surrey. Sir Francis agreed to the approach.

During dinner, Victoria received a call from Feng Wang of the *SCMP*. She answered, and Feng informed her that the police would announce tonight, that Bertrand Wilmington's death was now being treated as a homicide investigation. He asked whether Victoria had information to add since their earlier conversation. She explained the status of the case and confirmed the details he had.

About thirty minutes later, Victoria's phone buzzed. It was an alert from the *SCMP* app on her iPhone that Feng's article had been posted. As usual, the article was sharp, raised the right questions, and presented the case accurately. It read as follows:

> *It is now up to the police to shed some light on the events of that night and find out what led one or more murderers to take Bertrand Wilmington's life. BHS's inquiry should allow the SFC to look at the regulatory side of the events. The possible ramifications of the case in the Mainland remain to be seen; Bertrand Wilmington was in charge of important accounts of provincial agencies. Once again, the aggressive climate that permeates trading rooms may have been responsible. When the dust settles, BHS will certainly want to take corrective measures within its organization.*

"Smart and well informed," Sir Francis commented with a smile when he read the article. "Laura, let's have a conference call with our general counsel and the chairman after dinner, before the London office closes. We need to be sure there is no obstacle to your advisory. Victoria, please organize a meeting with Henry Chang at the crack of dawn tomorrow. And keep Diana Yu informed."

When Victoria arrived home, she immediately called Diana Yu. She was still in a meeting with the police commissioner. Half an hour later, she returned Victoria's call.

"Congratulations," Diana began.

"I feel good," Victoria admitted. "I believe we'll find the truth. What about your side?"

"Everything is in place. Let's hope the media won't be too harsh."

"Have you read Feng Wang's piece in the *SCMP*?"

"I just read it. He's honest and well informed. But I hate when the media interfere with our investigations. It can be counterproductive."

"Do you know if the police intend to interrogate Bertrand's parents?" Victoria asked.

"We discussed this. Their testimony is so central to the evidence that we will, at some stage, want to talk to them. Why?"

"We're in touch with them." Victoria explained the details Christine had discussed with them. "They are relieved to know that their son didn't commit suicide but alarmed by the possible consequences of a criminal investigation. Is there any way they could be interrogated early? They would like to escape to their house in Surrey as soon as possible. They don't need the aggravation of a media frenzy and photographers."

"I will look into it tomorrow. It might be difficult since their testimony is so critical. Until the inquiry is concluded, I doubt that they will be allowed to leave."

"Could you be at our office tomorrow morning at eight? We'd like to try to persuade Henry to tell us what he knows and to surrender voluntarily to the police. If that's too difficult for you, please bring in a member of the criminal department."

"I will be there tomorrow at eight with a member of the criminal team," Diana promised.

37

When Olivia Shuler informed David Chen that he was expected to join a meeting the next morning at the bank, he was furious. He demanded to know who had called the meeting. When he heard that it was Harvey Lee, he almost had a heart attack. What was this about? What would he tell his family? At first, he refused to go, but as he cooled down, he realized that to do so would be to admit guilt. He attempted to learn more from Olivia, but she was under strict instructions not to disclose the subject or the attendants of the meeting, and she held firm.

After David hung up, he booked himself on the only Cathay Pacific direct flight from Bali. He went back to the family lunch table and informed his wife, Claire, that he had been called into a meeting and would have to fly out in the afternoon but would be back the next evening. Claire frowned. It wasn't normal for David to have to handle office emergencies in person. When he mentioned Harvey Lee's name, she saw fear is his eyes. It was not the expression of the overachiever she was used to. Claire Wang was a magistrate at the Juvenile Court of Hong Kong, having formerly worked as an attorney at a Hong Kong law firm specializing in matrimonial and family law. She was good at reading people.

David's flight was scheduled to arrive in Hong Kong at 9:00 p.m., but a storm delayed the flight by several hours. He didn't land until 2:00 a.m. The six hours he spent at the airport were torture, but they gave him time to draw up plans for the bank's dealings with the SFC.

The improper trades he had directed had been a stupid mistake; he had only wanted to put pressure on Bertrand to have sex with him. Not that big a deal, David thought, and certainly nothing that would threaten his career. He might have to leave BHS, but he would immediately find a job. Wouldn't he? People who really understood the back office of fixed income were few, and those positions were as well paid as traders. This hadn't been the case in the past, but it was now given the integrity of the back office and its role in risk management, which were both so critical in the new regulatory environment.

David managed to get some sleep on the plane. But nothing had prepared him for the bomb that would explode in his hands when he opened his BlackBerry as the plane taxied to the gate. The *SCMP*'s breaking news alert popped up: "Police Launch Murder Inquiry into BHS Trader's Death."

What could have happened? Why on earth would the police have changed their ruling? Who was behind this? As his mind spun at a thousand miles an hour, David realized that there was no way he could escape becoming a suspect. At least Olivia had erased his personal e-mails. The police and the SFC would still have access to all his professional e-mails, but he hoped that any incriminating ones would be irretrievable. He was so grateful to Olivia. David also couldn't escape the SFC inquiry or the internal inquiry, but the latter would probably be more administrative than anything else.

David called his wife in the morning. She had just read the *SCMP* article and was concerned.

"Do you have anything to do with this Bertrand Wilmington?" Claire asked.

"I cleared his transactions. He ran the derivatives department."

"Will they interrogate you for the murder?"

"I don't think so," David said, unsure of the truth of his response.

"You were there the night of the murder, don't you remember? I was at the US consulate, and you called me to tell me that you would be at the office for several more hours. I even threw you out of bed that night; you were completely drunk. You slept on the sofa. Did you see anything?"

"No. We spent time reconciling some transactions that Bertrand and his team had badly input. It was all technical and complex. We had to unwind some transactions with the proprietary trading department. Some trades had been irregularly booked into a client's account."

"And then he committed suicide?" Claire yelled incredulously.

"I guess . . ."

"Do you really believe that this story will fly?! Are you kidding me? You are an absolutely irresponsible man, and now maybe even a criminal. I'm flying back this afternoon. I'll see you tonight."

David tried to tell her that there was no reason for her to shorten her vacation with their two children, but Claire hung up on him. She couldn't be fooled. She was absolutely livid that he wasn't being more honest with her. Perhaps he was in denial. It seemed a weak defense mechanism to her, and it made her furious.

Claire knew how prosecutors worked better than her husband did. He was afraid of her, not only because of her anger but also because his homosexuality might be revealed. If his secret became public, it could break up his family.

Of course, it was no secret to Claire. She had discovered David's sexual preferences after the birth of their twins. She had found e-mails on his phone. Nothing on the surface could have indicated his penchant for boys. She chose to ignore it and lived as though they had a normal marriage for the children. David did it to save face. There was part of her that still felt sympathy and gentleness for him, but his recent erratic behavior worried her.

38

At around 8 a.m. that morning, Sir Francis, Laura Woo, Christine, and Victoria were finishing their meeting at Pegasus.

When Henry Chang arrived for his appointment, Sir Francis joined Victoria. Laura had been authorized to advise the SFC and could no longer be part of this investigation. Henry was livid. He probably hadn't slept at all, and the *SCMP* article from the previous evening added even more stress. He was stunned to see Diana Yu in an adjacent meeting room.

"As you probably know," Sir Francis began, "The Hong Kong Police Department now considers Bertrand Wilmington's death a homicide."

"Yes. I read the *SCMP* piece. It was a relief to know that the truth might emerge. We owe it to Bertrand."

"Mr. Chang, what did you know about Bertrand's plans? You were his superior, if I am not mistaken."

Henry hesitated. "Technically yes, but we were more like partners. Which plans are you referring to?"

"Tell me what you know," Sir Francis insisted.

"I know he had plans to go back to Sydney in the future, but nothing was concrete or immediate. He still has some family there."

"You understand that the facts are critical. The Chongqing Hedge Fund managers told you to eliminate him. If we're asked to testify, we'll have to disclose the contents of your conversation with the fund managers in Shanghai. This is a serious matter. Based on the facts, you are one of the prime suspects. You need to tell us what you know."

Henry collapsed in his chair. He had never expected to be a murder suspect. His whole universe was unraveling before him, and neither his money nor his family could protect him from what was to come. He stood up, went to the door, and cast a furious glance at Victoria.

"You bitch. I withdraw my mandate to Pegasus. You set me up. I thought you would defend me."

This wasn't the first time that Victoria had seen Henry Chang upset. He was losing his senses, and that could be dangerous for him. Victoria knew she was the only person standing between Henry and his own self-destruction. As much as she hated it, she was not prepared to let him destroy himself.

"Don't leave, Henry. If you have done nothing wrong, we are probably the only ones who have the credibility to defend you. Do you want to finish the day in jail?"

Henry thought about it for a moment, and sat down again.

"Could you tell me why you hired Pegasus, and specifically me?"

"I knew I was in danger after the meeting in Shanghai and Bertrand's death. I didn't know about the risks from BHS, the anti-gay contingent, or the SFC. I should have told you everything I knew at the beginning. I thought the sexual orientation front was the least dangerous for me, so I launched you there. I felt squeezed on the three fronts. I could have helped Bertrand, but the threats from Shanghai were a reminder of the fragility of my position. I thought I was vulnerable before, but now I'm totally exposed, and nobody believes me any longer. Not even you."

"Are you responsible for Bertrand Wilmington's death?"

"Probably, by not acting. I should have realized earlier how evil

David Chen was. I should have pressed Bertrand to report to compliance immediately. Instead, I tried to cover my colleagues, and when Bertrand made the report, it was too late."

"Did you push him or incite him to commit suicide? Tell me the truth, Henry."

Victoria saw desperation in Henry's eyes. Nothing would move her. She needed the truth.

"Never. I liked Bertrand. He was like a younger brother to me. I truly wanted him to succeed. But I also protected the important Chongqing Hedge Fund from Bertrand's meddling. I was angry with him, but never to the point of wishing him ill."

Victoria dropped the bomb on Henry. "Bertrand had arranged to go back to the University of Sydney. He was not leaving to meet his family. He was looking forward to a new life with Louis Cheung. He was supposed to fly the week after he fell to his death."

"Oh my God." Henry shuddered in disbelief.

Henry was clearly devastated now that he knew his friend had been so close to realizing his dream. It was more than he could take. He couldn't speak. After a few minutes that seemed like a century, Victoria asked him whom he thought might have been responsible for Bertrand's death.

"Bertrand was not a big drinker. At office parties, he would maybe have a beer or a glass of wine but was always sober. That night, David Chen pressured Bertrand to drink. Bertrand mentioned that he didn't feel well. Maybe David even drugged him. Bertrand went and stood at the only working window, and he opened it to throw out his drink. I couldn't see him, but the next thing I heard was a piercing scream. I immediately ran toward the window and the scene I encountered was something that will haunt me forever: David Chen standing near the window, grinning with a disturbing look in his eyes. He will deny it, but that is what I saw. I didn't see him push Bertrand, but I'm convinced that he did. It will be extremely difficult to get him to admit to it."

Victoria put a hand on Henry's shoulder. He looked up at her with disbelief. He noticed a difference in her eyes. Now, she trusted him.

"You should have been more open with us. You will have to accept your part in this, and you know it. You might not have killed Bertrand, but you've put a number of people in danger. But you can do your part now, too. You must testify for your friend."

"Let me talk to Harvey Lee," Sir Francis said. "I'll tell him what you told us. He can't do anything now, but at least he'll trust our judgment. Now you're in the hands of the police, okay?"

Henry nodded. The ordeal was over. Better to confront reality than try to escape from it. Victoria left to brief Diana about this new information, and the two women returned to the meeting.

"What should I do with the police?" Henry asked Diana.

"We'll take you to headquarters. You need to take the initiative to tell us everything you know. My colleagues in the criminal department will talk to you about the murder, and I'll interrogate you about the fraud. A formal deposition will be required."

"I apologize, to both of you, for not telling the truth," Henry said sheepishly, but earnestly.

"Thank you," Victoria said. "But you can't apologize to one person: Bertrand Wilmington. You might not have killed him, but you may have been able to save him."

"This will forever be my burden." Henry sobbed.

The weight of what he had just said was clear. It didn't help that it would be tough for him to convince anybody of his innocence, and David Chen was unlikely to confess.

"When David is interrogated," Sir Francis said, "he will have to explain how these trades broke the Chinese wall between proprietary trading and client business. The SFC will also want to talk to John Highbridge about those trades. It's difficult to believe that what David might have initiated would have happened without the nod from John Highbridge. There is also no way your testimony alone will be strong enough in court to indict one or two of your colleagues. I'll call Harvey now to compare notes with Commissioner Chu and find out what repercussions this case might have in China."

The conversation and information about the next course of action relieved Henry. He was prepared to play his part, recognizing the risks associated with his position as the accusing witness. It would be a challenge for the police to prove David Chen's guilt beyond a reasonable doubt, but Henry would do everything he could.

39

Despite his worries, nothing could dissipate David Chen's feeling of accomplishment when he drove his bright yellow Lamborghini Gallardo into the BHS garage. He was on top of the universe and sure to be the center of attention. The media were there. He smiled and waved to them like a movie star. David's delusion about the situation couldn't be further from the truth.

The guards directed him to the senior executive garage, where none other than Mary Li met him.

"May I go to my office quickly?" David asked her. "I've got something to do. I need fifteen minutes."

"Fine, but I'll accompany you."

He had hoped to clean some documents, but that wouldn't be possible with Mary there. He was an outcast. It was the worst possible situation. BHS would not take responsibility for his fraud.

"Never mind. Let's go straight to the meeting." David put his arm around Mary's shoulder. She flinched and backed away.

Mary led David into the boardroom. A few minutes later, Harvey Lee and half a dozen colleagues entered. They switched on the video-conferencing system.

"Are we being taped?" David had naively thought this would be a meeting among colleagues on business matters. That was no longer the case.

"Yes," Harvey Lee said. "This is now a homicide investigation, so we need to take precautions. Taping our conversations on the subject is one of them."

"I hate it. This should just be among colleagues. I have nothing to hide, so I hoped we could resolve any misunderstanding privately."

The denial in David's tone exasperated Harvey Lee. How could a top executive believe that his pathetic attempt to distance himself from his responsibilities would be credible?

"Nothing to hide?" Harvey said. "Why did you instruct your assistant to delete the personal e-mails between you and Bertrand Wilmington?"

"I never did that. I wanted them to be put in a separate personal file in the system. Maybe she misunderstood."

"Did she express any resistance to do so?"

"She asked me to do it myself, but it wasn't safe for me to do it from Bali," he said, searching for an excuse.

"Which personal files did you want to erase?"

"I don't remember. Why is this important?"

"Because you are lying to us. If you had nothing to hide, then there was no reason to delete e-mails between you and your now deceased colleague. How could you have left on vacation the day after his death? Are you completely irresponsible?" Harvey Lee had impeccable control of his emotions until he was facing a disingenuous person. Nothing would stop him from getting to bottom of this now.

"You should know better," Harvey continued. "Your phone has been tapped since your meeting with Mary Li and Gregory Simpson. Not only did you behave as if you were above the rules, but you bullied Mary."

"Why does it matter?" David shrugged.

"The inquiry I launched, which was known to all executives of your rank, should have made you more careful. My memo clearly

instructed everyone to keep their IT equipment and contents unchanged. When you instructed Olivia to delete your e-mails, she
called Mary Li, and we duplicated your hard drive and your e-mails
that day."

"You can't do that! Those are private files." David felt increasingly
clawed at. Every excuse he tried backfired. How much did the bank
know?

"Nothing is private, David. You should know that. Do you remember the contents of those messages?"

"Vaguely. There was nothing special in them."

"Do you want me to refresh your memory and read some of them?"
Harvey asked sarcastically.

"No, please," David replied.

Harvey continued the barrage. "You sexually harassed Bertrand.
It's unmistakable. And you followed your threat with a series of trades
in which you violated our rules. You dumped HK$50 million of deriv-
atives into the Chongqing account without his consent."

"That's not true. You can't prove it!" David shouted desperately.

"Bertrand Wilmington informed Mary Li when the transaction
appeared. You might remember the meeting with John Highbridge
that followed. Bertrand never agreed to execute this trade and had to
report it to compliance."

"Bertrand is dead. You can't make a dead person testify."

"True. But we won't need his testimony. His electronic legacy
talks. And there were eight of you in your office, including Bertrand,
after the trade. Don't try to lie to us, David."

40

A POLICE CAR WAS WAITING FOR DIANA YU AND HENRY CHANG IN the Pegasus garage. They immediately hurried to police headquarters, entering through a side door to avoid the media.

Diana advised Henry to be completely candid. A uniformed policeman then led him to an interrogation room, where William Young, the head of the criminal department, was waiting with Henry's lawyer, Joseph Kindler. He wasn't exactly a criminal lawyer, but he was available.

"I'm here to tell you what I know," Henry said. "I'm not sure I know everything, but I want justice to prevail. My initial statement is unambiguous. I did not kill Bertrand Wilmington, either directly or indirectly. I perhaps could have prevented this dramatic event, but I had no part in his death."

"We are recording your testimony," Diana said. "We appreciate your candor. The fact that you didn't come forward sooner with this information is a matter for the prosecution. At this stage, we want to know what happened the night of Bertrand's death."

Henry continued. "We had received instruction from General Counsel Harvey Lee to settle the trades affecting Bertrand Wilmington's client, the Chongqing Hedge Fund. The meeting very quickly became acrimonious, and David Chen accused Bertrand of betraying him by going to compliance and audit. He said Bertrand wasn't a man and challenged him to drink. Bertrand wasn't used to alcohol. He became erratic. It is possible David pushed him."

Henry's eyes began to water as he recalled that dreadful moment. It was the moment for him to admit in front of Diana his responsibility for this drama.

"I should have intervened. David is a bully. None of us wanted to confront him. Bertrand opened the only window he could to throw out his alcohol. John and I continued to concentrate on the trades, and then we heard a scream. Bertrand had fallen out of the window. It was horrible. I can't be certain that David Chen pushed him. All I know is that he was alone with Bertrand, next to the open window, at the time of the fall."

As he remembered that tragic moment, Henry went silent. He could have stopped it. He and John had clearly underestimated how far David was willing to go. It hadn't occurred to Henry that anything serious could have happened. If they had done their duty, Bertrand would be alive and in Sydney. Henry couldn't bear his responsibility.

"Are you willing to sign your written testimony, Henry?"

"Yes. I owe it to Bertrand, whatever the consequences. Even if I have to go to jail, I prefer to have a clear conscience. I'll have to live with my cowardice. I'm ready."

Henry was distraught as he waited for his statement to be typed. The head of the criminal department left the room, called the prosecutor, and asked for an arrest mandate charging David Chen with murder, fraud, sexual harassment, and destruction of evidence.

"We cannot let David go free," William Young, head of the criminal department said. "The only way we will be able to conduct this investigation is if he is arraigned. Keep me posted."

As soon as the mandate arrived, Young and Diana went to BHS headquarters.

41

THE ATMOSPHERE IN THE LEGAL DEPARTMENT ROOM WAS TENSE. Despite Harvey Lee's hard questioning, David Chen denied every accusation. Victoria then got a text from Harvey Lee. "Come up and join us."

She showed the message to Sir Francis, who nodded and told her to comply.

"Let me introduce Victoria Leung," Harvey said. "She is a senior detective at Pegasus and has to ask you a few questions about the Chongqing Hedge Fund."

Victoria was everything David hated in a woman: honest, assertive, strong, and, most of all, not submissive.

"Get her out of my face!" David yelled. "All this happened because of girls."

"What do you mean?" Victoria asked.

"Olivia Schuler betrayed me. I thought she would be loyal to me. You two plotted against me!"

"Are you referring to the e-mails?" Harvey Lee asked.

"Yes. Girls can't be trusted -"

"But they can be bullied," Victoria interrupted. "Do you know Wieslaw Mysliwski?"

"Yes, he works for the fixed-income department. That's what I call a loyal guy."

"Why did you send him to attack Louis Cheung at the Macau restaurant?"

"I didn't," David yelled.

He was now visibly angry, and the allusion to Louis Cheung had only infuriated him more.

Victoria looked him straight in the eye. "What did you have against Bertrand? What did he do to you?"

"He rejected me," David responded coldly.

"How?"

"When he went to audit to talk about the Chongqing Hedge Fund, it was too much. He had found out about the phantom account and was stupid enough to tell me and Henry."

Harvey Lee took over. "And you falsified the account number?"

"Absolutely not. Everything was legitimate," David contested.

"You photocopied the real account documents and kept them for our records, but the originals that you sent to the legal department were different. We checked them in London."

"Shit." David muttered to himself. "What does that prove?"

"The CSRC arrested the account managers after Henry met them the day before Bertrand's death. They told the CSRC that you had managed to falsify the accounts. Do you know why Henry flew to Shanghai?" Harvey asked.

"He went to meet the client," David responded.

Harvey continued. "They had discovered that Bertrand knew of the phantom account, and they wanted Henry to liquidate Bertrand. You and Henry are the ones who falsified the documents."

"How did you find out?" David erupted.

Despite his impeccable appearance, David had become furious. He could feel the claws digging in. He desperately needed to find an escape.

"I found it," Victoria said. "I worked at CITIC, so I know that all agency accounts from Mainland provinces have the same structure. You think you could hide a hyphen from us?"

"That proves nothing."

"It proves that you created a corrupt intermediate account and, with Henry Chang, put together a system to defraud the Chongqing Hedge Fund," Harvey Lee said. "Why did you do it?"

"It was the only way we could get the account. Henry Chang was perfectly aware of the situation. If he was told to eliminate Bertrand, why don't you interrogate him? You have too many naive players at BHS, sir."

"Naive or simply honest?" Harvey interjected.

Victoria could sense that David was on the verge of breaking down and desperately wanted it to happen. She took a risk. "Why did you want to attack Louis Cheung?"

"Because he was Bertrand's lover. He needed to be taught a lesson. I've wanted to do that since we were at the University of Hong Kong."

"Wieslaw and his two accomplices have been arrested. They told the police the attack was your idea. Did the Chongqing fund managers ask you to do it?" Victoria asked.

"They had nothing to do with that."

"And with Bertrand's death?"

"Definitely not. I controlled *them*. I had them eating out of my hand," David said.

"Louis was badly hurt. The police will go after you for this."

"Why should I care? I didn't touch Louis Cheung."

"Have you ever heard of conspiracy, David?" Harvey asked. "You are as guilty as they are."

"And the woman who was assaulted," Victoria felt her anger rising. "You sent the trio to attack her too? You are a coward."

"The last thing I expected was for a woman to be with Louis."

"Then why did they attack her?" Victoria yelled.

"That woman had no business being there. She got what she deserved!" David shouted.

"I am that woman," Victoria said quietly. "I was meeting with Louis to learn more about Bertrand and his tragic death."

Victoria had dealt a lethal blow. David couldn't escape. A murderous look appeared in his eyes and his true violent nature could no longer remain hidden.

"You bitch! I should have killed you instead of Bertrand. Girls like you shouldn't be allowed to have any power. Do you seriously think you're doing any good? You will never prove anything."

The silence that followed his statement was stunning. When David finally realized that he had confessed, he became hysterical. He pounded the table with his fists and screamed, "I hate you! I'll never admit anything to the police. She tricked me," he leaped toward Victoria, in an attempt to hurt her. "She made me say it!"

At that moment, a man burst into the interrogation room and grabbed David by the collar. "I am William Young, head of the criminal department of the Hong Kong Police Force. I heard everything that was said. We suspected that you had the best opportunity to push Bertrand Wilmington. And now your last statement is an acknowledgment of your guilt."

42

WHAT HARVEY LEE HAD NOT DISCLOSED WAS THAT IN THE CON-
ference room of the legal department, members of the Hong Kong
Police Force, the SFC, and Pegasus had assembled. They had seen the
entire show on video.

David Chen was visibly shaken and clearly could not come to
grips with what he had just done. Three women—Olivia Schuler,
Diana Yu, and Victoria Leung—had managed to tear down his façade.

"Henry Chang was with me!" David said. "The three of us were by
the window. I am not the only one who pushed Bertrand."

"You drugged Bertrand, and your colleagues were not near the
window. Henry is testifying to the police as we speak."

William Young stood up and read the warrant. "David Chen, you
are under arrest for murder, fraud, sexual harassment, and multiple
infractions of securities regulations. You have the right to remain
silent. Everything you say can be used against you. You are entitled
to legal assistance."

David was a zombie. He remained still until a uniformed officer
handcuffed him. The group went to his office on the twenty-second
floor. Olivia Schuler was there when they entered.

An officer emptied David's pockets and handed his keys, passes, and phones to Olivia. An ocean of sadness appeared in her eyes.

"I tried to warn you, David. Why didn't you listen?"

He looked with desperation at his assistant of five years. "I have been betrayed by women all my life. Please call Claire. Tell her to stay in Bali." He paused. "Tell her I apologize and wish her well. Tell her to forget about me."

The trading room was dead silent. As David was escorted out of the room, the traders and salesmen stood up one by one and turned their backs on him. Everybody had liked Bertrand Wilmington, an honest and decent man. The coming weeks and months would be tough for them. Their department's reputation had been badly wounded.

Once outside, David was pushed into a police car and taken to headquarters. On the way to the interrogation, he saw Henry Chang sitting in another office. Everything was clear. What he needed now was a very good lawyer.

"I'd like to call my lawyer."

The officer showed him to the phone.

He called Bernie Kravis, a friend who had helped him to stay out of trouble in matters of securities regulation in the past.

"Bernie, I've been arrested for murder and securities fraud. Can you come to police headquarters?"

"I'm in a meeting, David, but I'll send one of my Hong Kong colleagues who specializes in criminal litigation."

"Thank you."

Fifteen minutes later, Shirley Wu, a reputed member of the Hong Kong Bar, entered and asked to speak with David Chen in private. He explained the events to her.

William Young entered and explained that Prosecutor Zhan had arrived. They went to the prosecution room.

Olivia called David's wife.

"David has been arrested," she told Claire.

"Oh my God!" Claire gasped.

"Don't go online or speak to the media. We can't control what will be said or published," Olivia warned.

After a moment, Claire responded. "I need to protect the children. I understand that I'll be better off staying put until the court reopens after its recess. In the back of my mind, I always worried that something like this could happen, but never actually thought David would be arrested."

"David is accused of the murder of Bertrand Wilmington. He has asked me to convey his apologies to you and hopes that you and the kids do your best to forget about him."

A long silence followed. Claire began to sob.

"Thank you, Olivia. I need to take care of the kids now."

"I've booked a flight to Bali for tomorrow," Olivia said. "You and I need to go over a few important personal details about what will happen in the next few weeks."

"That is very kind of you. Unless you hear from me, I will see you tomorrow."

43

Victoria informed Christine about the arrest, and Christine called Bertrand's parents.

"David Chen, the head of the back office at BHS, was arrested this morning. It appears that he has confessed to Bertrand's murder."

"Oh my God," Christopher and Catherine gasped.

A few moments passed as they digested the news and considered what it meant for them.

"May we leave for Britain tonight?" Christopher asked.

"Wait a day until I get confirmation that your testimony will not be needed," Christine replied.

"Don't tell us anything else. We are so heartbroken already. The best we can do is go to Surrey for some time alone. Thank you so much for what you've done."

The loss of their child, the murder, and everything that surrounded the death was more than the Wilmingtons could bear.

The phone rang in Ian Adler's office. The caller ID indicated that it was the direct line of James Liu, his counterpart at the CSRC in Shanghai.

"Good afternoon, Ian. I saw that the police arrested one of the

BHS executives. Does this have anything with what we discussed in Shanghai?"

"Yes," Ian responded. "David Chen set up the fraudulent Chongqing Hedge Fund account."

"How did you find out?" James asked.

"He and Henry Chang signed the account's opening documents. The photocopy kept in Hong Kong was forged with a different account number. Our forensic analysis proves it. I assume that David will try to limit his jail time for murder and will admit his wrongdoing to us."

"Murder?" James asked, surprised.

"Yes. He has confessed to killing Bertrand Wilmington."

"I have an important request from Beijing that I need to share with you," James continued. "We would like to avoid any further publicity about the misbehavior of the Chongqing municipality. We have arrested the managers of the Chongqing Hedge Fund."

"I understand. Frankly, I cannot give you full reassurance. However, in our preliminary discussions, we all agree that it is in nobody's interest to see a trial in this case. We hope that David Chen will also see it this way. If the case goes to trial, the issue of sexual harassment will be disclosed."

"What do you mean?"

"David is gay. So was Bertrand. David had been harassing him," Ian explained.

"I didn't know that side of the story."

"That will not affect what the SFC will do, although it gives us leverage in obtaining a guilty plea."

"We would greatly appreciate it if the Hong Kong authorities could avoid a trial," James said. "We are handling our side of the problem ourselves; we do not need extra visibility."

"I hear you loud and clear," Ian agreed.

"Thank you, Ian. I will make sure Beijing understands it and does not move before the SAR has better visibility."

Henry Chang had been subjected to ten hours of interrogation by successive police departments. But the most painful was the last hour with two representatives of the financial fraud department. They took a break around 8 p.m. to let him have a sandwich.

At 8:30 p.m., Diana Yu joined them and resumed grilling Henry about the proprietary trades and the Chongqing Hedge Fund.

"I tried to support Bertrand as much as I could," Henry continued. "But I was afraid of David Chen. He had a part in the Oriental Real Estate IPO conspiracy. He never forgave me for not having been fined for my role in the Oriental Finance cover-up. Since the financial crisis, his power has increased, and he could accuse just about anyone of misbehaving. He even used his power to eliminate some executives."

"Nobody fought back?" Diana asked.

"Mary is the only one who did. I was absolutely sure he would have her fired after she confronted him in the meeting we had two days before Bertrand's death."

Henry should have confronted David and wouldn't. Diana thought to herself. *What a coward.*

"Why did you go to the emergency meeting in Shanghai?" Diana asked.

"When the managers of the Chongqing Hedge Fund realized that Bertrand knew he was dealing with a corrupt account, they called me immediately. They were absolutely furious and said that if Bertrand was still on the account in one week, they would have to deal with him."

"Did you tell Bertrand?" Diana inquired.

"I did, but I advised him to wait until I returned to do anything," Henry lamented. "I should have advised him to go straight to audit and compliance. He would still be alive if I had."

As the interrogation continued, further proof of Henry's cowardice and lack of authority emerged. He wanted to resolve problems internally and felt that, by going through audit and compliance, he would be betraying his colleagues. Bertrand, on the other hand, was brave.

At the end of the conversation, the police officers involved convened to decide Henry's fate. He had given them what they had needed to arrest David Chen, but Henry had committed fraud.

"He must be put under house arrest," Diana decided. "We can't know how David Chen's allies will react. For his protection and ours, we should keep Henry in jail for the next 72 hours."

Everybody agreed: the risks of letting Henry go free were too high. If anything happened, they would all be in trouble. A member of the criminal department went back to the interrogation room with Diana and explained the situation to Henry.

As much as he hated it, Henry recognized that he probably did need the protection. No one knew what could happen, and he might be forever in danger in Hong Kong. After shooting Diana a sad smile, he followed the police officer out of the room.

Diana left police headquarters and informed Victoria of the results of the interrogation. They decided to meet at Victoria's apartment for a nightcap. They both needed to relieve the pressure of this terrible day. Victoria opened the door in her bathrobe and hugged her friend.

"Henry finally told us everything he knew," Diana explained. "He still doesn't grasp the full picture. We probably would have had no case against him if he hadn't hid information from us. He can be so nice one minute and so manipulative and sneaky the next. He should know better after the Oriental Finance problems."

"Where is he now?" Victoria asked.

"We're keeping him for 72 hours for his own protection. After that we will probably put him under house arrest."

"Will there be a trial?"

"Everything depends on David. If he pleads guilty, it will just be a half-day in court, and the judge will send him to jail. It will be best for everyone if that happens."

"David acted so erratically this morning," said Victoria. "He completely lost his balance. I made him so furious that he actually said that he wished he would have killed me instead of Bertrand." Victoria took a breath. "How do you feel about Henry now?"

Diana took a moment before responding. "I need a man who has true inner strength. Henry is spineless. This has been a very difficult experience, but I am so relieved that we were never engaged. I was really in love with him once, but he betrayed me in a number of ways. The request to hire you was the last straw."

"I'm so glad you're out of that relationship," said Victoria.

Before long, Diana fell asleep, and Victoria put a blanket over her before retiring to her own room.

As she looked out the window, the lights of the city glowed in Kowloon Bay. It was glamorously glittering and peaceful at the same time. She barely read three pages of her magazine before falling into a deep sleep. The sunrise finally woke her.

Victoria shuffled into the living room and gazed at Diana, still fast asleep. Victoria was moved. Her friend looked as if she had been fighting monsters. At least this time Victoria and Diana had won the battle. It was time for a hot jasmine tea.

Epilogue

DAVID CHEN'S LAWYER, SHIRLEY WU, MANAGED TO CONVINCE HIM to plead guilty and to persuade the judge that the murder had not been premeditated. David was sentenced to thirty years in prison.

BHS was fined HK$1 billion for default of surveillance and infractions of proprietary trading regulations.

The CSRC liquidated the Chongqing Hedge Fund, and a Chongqing court sentenced each of the three hedge fund managers to twenty years in prison. The beneficiaries of the fraud were never publicly disclosed.

At the end of the summer, Christopher and Catherine Wilmington returned from Britain and resumed their cultural and charitable activities on the island. They never had to testify and were kept out of the proceedings.

Claire and David Chen agreed to divorce, and she got custody of the children. She resumed her duties at the juvenile court after demonstrating to the Supreme Court that she had nothing to do with her husband's deeds.

Henry Chang was fined an undisclosed amount by the Hong Kong SFC and got a suspended jail sentence of three years. He was barred from exercising financial services responsibilities for ten years.

He left Hong Kong after the judicial decision and returned to the UK, where he decided to join his father's shipping business. He continued to live between London and Hong Kong.

Diana got promoted at the Hong Kong Police Force.

Louis Cheung did eventually go to Sydney. He confronted his attackers from the restaurant, and, with the help of Victoria's testimony, the gang of three each received a fixed five-year jail term. This time, the prosecution did not dare minimize the gravity of the case.

Laura Woo invited Victoria to a seafood restaurant for lunch.

"Let me congratulate you, Victoria. You did an impeccable job throughout the investigation. The Flying Dragon has certainly earned another stripe. More importantly, you've earned everyone's respect."

"The cost was high," Victoria said, "but I'm glad to have seen it through. I could use a holiday now."

"I might need your help on another financial case. Are you interested in working together?"

"Who's the client?"

"Harvey Lee. He insists that you and I team up for this one. He wants us to advise him on the clean-up of the fixed-income department."

They both smiled. It was an amazing opportunity. After lunch, Victoria reflected on the merits and pitfalls of her job. She decided that she thoroughly enjoyed it and was looking forward to the firm debriefing in London at the next partners' meeting. "The unexpected always happens" was Sir Francis's favorite statement. It had certainly been true in this case. And it would undoubtedly be the true in the future.

CPSIA information can be obtained at www.ICGtesting.com
Printed in the USA
LVOW11s1500100316

478624LV00001B/202/P